W9-CCD-427

NEGIMA!

Ken Akamatsu

TRANSLATED BY
Hajime Honda

ADAPTED BY
Peter David and Kathleen O'Shea David

LETTERED BY
Studio Cutie

DEL REY

BALLANTINE BOOKS • NEW YORK

A Word from the Author

Hi, this is Ken Akamatsu. It's been a while.

After taking over a year off after *Love Hina*, I have returned to work with my new serial, *Magister Negi Magi*! I hope you enjoy it.

The protagonist of *Negima!*, Negi, is cute, smart and talented—the kind of protagonist you'd never find in my previous manga! Ironically enough, though, top student personalities like him don't usually stand out (ha ha)!

So, are you gonna take the plunge!?

It's been so long.

The 31 beautiful girls in his class all have unique personalities, each with her share of trials and tribulations. (Actually, some of them aren't even human. . . .) Maybe they're the real protagonists of *Negima!*?

So let's take our time and watch over Negi as he grows up.

Ken Akamatsu
http://www.ailove.net

Translator—Hajime Honda
Adaptors—Peter David and Kathleen O'Shea David
Lettering—Studio Cutie
Cover Design—David Stevenson

This is a work of fiction. Any resemblance to actual persons, living or dead, is unintentional and purely coincidental.

A Del Rey® Book
Published by The Random House Publishing Group

Copyright © 2004 Ken Akamatsu. All rights reserved.
This publication-rights arranged through Kodansha, Ltd.

All rights reserved under International and Pan-American Copyright Conventions. Published in the United States by The Random House Publishing Group, a division of Random House, Inc., New York, and simultaneously in Canada by Random House of Canada Limited, Toronto. First published in serial form by Shonen Magazine Comics and subsequently published in book form by Kodansha, Ltd., Tokyo in 2003. Copyright © 2003 by Ken Akamatsu.

Del Rey is a registered trademark and the Del Rey colophon is a trademark of Random House, Inc.

www.delreydigital.com

Library of Congress Control Number: 2004090830

ISBN 0-345-47046-X

Manufactured in the United States of America

First Edition: May 2004

10 9 8 7 6 5 4 3 2 1

Honorifics

Throughout the Del Rey Manga books, you will find Japanese honorifics left intact in the translations. For those not familiar with how the Japanese use honorifics, and more important, how they differ from American honorifics, we present this brief overview.

Politeness has always been a critical facet of Japanese culture. Ever since the feudal era, when Japan was a highly stratified society, use of honorifics—which can be defined as polite speech that indicates relationship or status—has played an essential role in the Japanese language. When addressing someone in Japanese, an honorific usually takes the form of a suffix attached to one's name (example: "Asuna-san"), or as a title at the end of one's name or in place of the name itself (example: "Negi-sensei," or simply "Sensei!").

Honorifics can be expressions of respect or endearment. In the context of manga and anime, honorifics give insight into the nature of the relationship between characters. Many translations into English leave out these important honorifics, and therefore distort the "feel" of the original Japanese. Because Japanese honorifics contain nuances that English honorifics lack, it is our policy at Del Rey not to translate them. Here, instead, is a guide to some of the honorifics you may encounter in Del Rey Manga.

-san: This is the most common honorific, and is equivalent to Mr., Miss, Ms., Mrs., etc. It is the all-purpose honorific and can be used in any situation where politeness is required.

-sama: This is one level higher than *san*. It is used to confer great respect.

-dono: This comes from the word *tono*, which means *lord*. It is an even higher level than *sama*, and confers utmost respect.

-kun: This suffix is used at the end of boys' names to express familiarity or endearment. It is also sometimes used by men among friends, or when addressing someone younger or of a lower station.

-chan: This is used to express endearment, mostly toward girls. It is also used for little boys, pets, and even among lovers. It gives a sense of childish cuteness.

Sempai: This title suggests that the addressee is one's "senior" in a group or organization. It is most often used in a school setting, where underclassmen refer to their upperclassmen as "sempai." It can also be used in the workplace, such as when a newer employee addresses an employee who has seniority in the company.

Kohai: This is the opposite of *sempai*, and is used toward underclassmen in school or newcomers in the workplace. It connotes that the addressee is of lower station.

Sensei: Literally meaning "one who has come before," this title is used for teachers, doctors, or masters of any profession or art.

-[blank]: Usually forgotten in these lists, but perhaps the most significant difference between Japanese and English. The lack of honorific means that the speaker has permission to address the person in a very intimate way. Usually, only family, spouses, or very close friends have this kind of permission. Known as *yobisute*, it can be gratifying when someone who has earned the intimacy starts to call one by one's name without an honorific. But when that intimacy hasn't been earned, it can also be very insulting.

魔法先生ネギま!
MAGISTER NEGI MAGI
1
赤松健
NEO HORIZON

Contents

1st Period—The Kid Instructor Is a Magician! 3

2nd Period—Panic in the Library!? 74

3rd Period—Bathhouse Rub ♥ 101

4th Period—The Dreaded Afterschool Session! 121

5th Period—Super Dodge Ball Competition!! Go Girls! (Part One) 141

6th Period—Super Dodge Ball Competition!! Go Girls! (Part Two) 159

Letter from the Editor 179

About the Creator 180

Character Sketches 181

Translation Notes 187

Preview of *Negima!* Volume 2 190

WHEN I CALL YOUR NAME, MY SORCEROUS GRADUATES...
TAKE YOUR MYSTIC DIPLOMA THAT WILL DICTATE YOUR CAREER.
AND REMEMBER: A CHARMED LIFE IS A HAPPY LIFE.
NEGI SPRINGFIELD! YOUR DIPLOMA!
YES SIR!
HUH...
OH, NO WAY!
WHERE IS YOUR TRAINING ASSIGNMENT?
IT'S ABOUT TO SHOW UP NOW.
HOW ABOUT YOU, NEGI?
I'M TO BE A FORTUNE TELLER IN LONDON!

FOM...
A TEACHER IN JAPAN
Negi Springfield
2003.07
LET'S SEE...
YOU'RE GOING TO BE...
... ...
MAAAAGUSSS!!!
BESIDES, HE'S JUST A SHRIMP! AND A SPACE CADET!
BUT HE'S ONLY TEN! THIS HAS TO BE SOME KIND OF MISTAKE!
A TEACHER. YES, I KNOW.
MAGUS! NEGI'S DIPLOMA SAYS HE'S TO BE—

THE DIPLOMA HAS SPOKEN.
NOT EVEN I, THE MAGUS, CAN SAY OTHERWISE.
DEDICATE YOURSELF, NEGI.
JAPAN'S YOUTH IS COUNTING ON YOU.
O-OH...
FOO...
SI-SISTER.
WORRY NOT. AN OLD FRIEND OF MINE RUNS THE SCHOOL.
HE, AND YOUR HEART, WILL GUIDE YOU.
I HAVE EVERY CONFIDENCE.
...
HM...
YES SIR!
I WILL !!

NEO HORIZON
NEGIMA!

O
RIZON
MAHORA
NEGIMA!

THROUGH HERE!
ALL TRAINS!
WHERE THE HECK IS TRACK ONE?!?
1·2

THIS IS A WORK OF FICTION. ANY RESEMBLANCE TO ACTUAL PERSONS, LIVING OR DEAD, IS UNINTENTIONAL AND PURELY COINCIDENTAL.

AH CHOO!
MUH... A-AH... AH...
HAVE YOU EVER? GOTTEN OFF, I MEAN?
TEE HEE
クス
クス
YOU SHOULD HAVE GOTTEN OFF LAST STOP.
I... I'M NOT SURE WHAT YOU...
ふわっ
FWOOSH
あっ
WHAT TH--?!
ACKKK!
HEY, WE'RE HERE.
NEXT STOP, MAHORA ACADEMY CENTRAL STATION.
A DIRTY MIND, I'M THINKING.
WHERE'D THAT BREEZE COME FROM?
OOPS...
プシュー
FSSSH
BYE, HONEY! ENJOY YOUR FUTURE RIDES! ❤
HUH?
STOP TEASING HIM!
IGNORE HER!
SHE'S A DOPE!
FWOOSH!

TUMP
TUMP
WELCOME BACK, STUDENTS! THE STUDENT COUNSELING COMMITTEE HAS DECLARED THIS PUNCTUALITY WEEK! TEN MINUTES UNTIL FIRST BELL! LATENESS WILL NOT BE TOLERATED!
RRRRRRRRRRRR
WE'RE LATE.
ALL YOURS.
GIMME A YAKISOBA ROLL!
LATE--
SO THIS IS WHAT JAPANESE SCHOOLS ARE LIKE?
WE'RE LATE.
WE'RE LATE.
HURRY!
EXCUSE ME! COULD SOMEONE TELL ME WHERE THE--

MOVE! MOVE!!
RRRRRRRRRRRR
HURRY.
HURRY.
ANYONE LATE THIS WEEK WILL RECEIVE A YELLOW CARD, SO WE URGE YOU TO BE AT SCHOOL AS EARLY AS POSSIBLE...
TMP
I CAN'T BE LATE ON THE VERY FIRST DAY!
OH NO. I'LL BE LATE.

THIS IS NUTS! WE CAN'T GREET THIS NEW TEACHER...
...AND MAKE IT TO CLASS AT THE SAME TIME!
WHY IS THE DEAN MAKING YOU DO THIS, ANYWAY?
'CAUSE I'M HIS GRAND-DAUGHTER.
WELL, IF THIS NEW TEACHER IS YOUR GRAMP'S PAL, HE MUST BE AN OLD FART.
MAYBE NOT. YOUR HOROSCOPE SAYS YOU'LL HAVE A FATEFUL ENCOUNTER TODAY.
TMP
TMP
TMP
TMP
NO, REALLY !?
IT'S RIGHT HERE, ASUNA.
IT ALSO SAYS IF YOU SPEAK YOUR LOVE'S NAME FIVE TIMES AND BARK, HE'S YOURS.
AW-RIGHT!

ARF!!!
TAKAHATA-SENSEI
TAKAHATA-SENSEI
TAKAHATA-SENSEI
TAKAHATA-SENSEI
TAKAHATA-SENSEI
...
URRK
GRR...
WOW, ASUNA, I'M REALLY IMPRESSED.
I DIDN'T EXPECT YOU TO ACTUALLY DO IT...
BECAUSE I'M SO DEDICATED TO TAKAHATA-SENSEI....?
NO, 'CAUSE YOU'RE SO GULLIBLE. I MADE IT UP, CHEESE HEAD.
KONOKA !!
ARGH
WHAT, CAN'T YOU TAKE A JOKE?
OH, I'LL TAKE MORE THAN TH–
WHOOSH
HUH?
WOOM
TP
TP
TP

KLAKETTY
ガッチャ
KI
AK
ガッチャ
SORRY TO BUTT IN...
...I JUST THOUGHT YOU SHOULD KNOW, YOU'LL BE HEART-BROKEN.

HUH...
IT'S JUST THAT, I'M KIND OF PSYCHIC, AND YOUR FUTURE—
NUH-NUH-NOT SO MUCH!
HOW'D YOU LIKE TO BE BROKEN?!
よろ...
FWOM...
...HEART-BRO-KEN?
OF ALL THE...
IS THAT A THREAT?!
I WAS JUST TRYING TO HELP/ TO WARN YOU—!
YOUR FUTURE'S LOOKING PRETTY SHORT! LIKE YOU!
YANK
AIEE
CRYING OUT LOUD! THERE'S AN IDEA!
C'MON, ASUNA, HE'S JUST A KID, FOR CRYING OUT LOUD.
HE'S SO CUTE.
ポポポ
BLINK BLINK
ワナワナ
GRRRR
くねぎぎぎぎ...
YAAAANK
TAKE BACK WHAT YOU SAID, TWERP!
ARGH
AIEEE
SO HOW'D THAT ANGER MANAGEMENT CLASS WORK OUT, ASUNA?

LOOK, KID: YOU GOT OFF AT THE WRONG STOP. THIS IS MAHORA SCHOOL DISTRICT. IT'S ALL GIRLS, OKAY?
THE ELEMENTARY SCHOOL'S ONE STOP BACK.
RIGHT. NOW APOLO-GIZE...
IF YOU DO, I'LL PUT YOU IN THE TRAIN INSTEAD OF UNDER IT.
I... JUST HAVE TO ASK...
ARE ALL JAPANESE GIRLS THIS CRANKY, OR DO YOU JUST HAVE REALLY SERIOUS ISSUES?
OHHH, THIS WON'T END WELL...
THAT'S IT! YOU LITTLE-!!
OKAY! OKAY! I'M SORRY!!
WELL WELL, ASUNA!

MAKING FRIENDS AGAIN, I S–
NEGI?! IS THAT YOU?!
"NEGI?" WHO'S–?
POINK
SMALL WORLD!
"YOU NUT?!"
WHERE– HOW– WHO–?
FSSSH
TA-TAKAHATA-SENSEI!?
MORNING, TAK--
TAKAMICHI! YOU NUT! HOW'S IT GOIN'!
I...I DIDN'T... UH... HE...
I SEE THE WELCOMING COMMITTEE FOUND YOU.
GLAD TO HAVE YOU ABOARD.
"NEGI-SENSEI." WHO'D'VE THOUGHT?
DID... DID HE...
...JUST CALL YOU ...?
...
NEGI-SENSEI? WHY... YES.
AHEM

ペコッ
BOW
MY NAME IS NEGI SPRINGFIELD...
...I'M YOUR NEW ENGLISH PROFESSOR.
I'LL-
-KILL HIM.

HE'D HAVE TO BE, WOULDN'T HE!
CALM DOWN, ASUNA. HE'S BRIGHTER THAN HE APPEARS.
YOU'RE JUST A LITTLE BRAT.
WHAT KIND OF STUPID JOKE IS THIS!
THAT'S "BRAT-SENSEI"... UH, I MEAN—
WONK
HU-WHAT?
YOU'LL FIND OUT YOURSELF, SINCE HE'S TAKING OVER MY CLASS.
YES! BREAK MY— HEY!
BREAK YOUR HEART?
YOU'RE NOT SERIOUS, TAKAHATA-SENSEI! IF...IF HE REPLACED YOU, IT WOULD...
OF ALL THE UNFAIR, UNREASONABLE... YOU NIT! YOU NOTHING! YOU—
GRRR
SHUT UP! WHO ASKED YOU!!!
AH CHOO
AH...
HM...
AH...
GRRRRR
I THINK... I'M ALLERGIC TO CRITICISM.

SNIPP
SNIPP
FWOOOSH
UH...
OOPS.
WHAT!?
HAS THIS WHOLE SCHOOL GONE MENTAL?!?
ぷん ぷん
SHLUMP
ぺたんっ
WOOL BEAR PANTIES...
UH HUH
うん
ふーっ
HAHH
BEAR PANTIES...

キーンコーン...
BONG
BONG...
HEAD-MASTER, PLEASE...
TELL ME THIS IS A MISTAKE, OR A JOKE.
IF YOU WISH, BUT IT WOULD BE LYING. SO, "PROFES-SOR"...
...YOUR TEACHING POST...
フォ HM
フォ HM
...SHOULD BE QUITE A CHALLENGE IN YOUR TRAINING, EH?

YES SIR.
YOU'LL STUDENT TEACH UNTIL MARCH...
DO BETTER THAN THAT.
YES, SIR.
I'LL DO MY BEST, SIR.
?
TRAINING?
WONK
HOLD ON, HERE.
THANKS LORDS, GRAND-PA.
BY THE WAY, MY GRAND-DAUGHTER IS AVAIL-ABLE...
...IF YOU REQUIRE A GIRL-FRIEND.
...BUT FOR ME TO. AND I DO...
IT IS NOT FOR YOU TO ACCEPT, ASUNA...
GRRRR
HM
HM
HM
IT'S... IT'S TOTALLY UNACCEPT-ABLE!!!
HELLOOO! THIS IS ME, STILL NOT BUYING A KID FOR A TEACHER!
...THERE WILL BE NO SECOND CHANCES. CLEAR?
...FOR NOW. BUT NEGI, IF YOU FAIL YOUR TRAINING...
...EXCEPT ...I WON'T. THAT'S ALL. I WON'T FAIL.
CRYSTAL, SIR. IF I FAIL...

CHAK
SHIZUNA-KUN! ARE YOU THERE?
YES SIR.
YOUR ADVISOR WILL BE SHIZUNA-SENSEI.
WE'LL START YOU OFF TODAY.
HA! JUST WHAT I WISHED TO HEAR.
OOF
WOOMF
SO... ANY QUES-TIONS?
I BET.
HELLO. YOU MUST BE THE FAMED NEGI.
CAN I...
...HAVE A COOKIE?
OH, YES, ONE MORE THING.
SHIZUNA HAS BEEN KEPT ABREAST OF THE SITUATION.

KONOKA, ASUNA-CHAN: WE'RE SHORT ON SPACE. SO NEGI-KUN WILL BUNK IN WITH YOU FOR NOW.
UGH
HUH?!
THAT'S FINE.
AW, HE'D BE LIKE A KID BROTHER.
HOW'S THAT A GOOD THING?!
WE'RE SUPPOSED TO LEARN FROM HIM AND WET NURSE HIM!? THIS IS—
HM HM
GRRRR...
うぐっ...
IT'S SETTLED.
ふいっ
HMPH
むっ
HUH

IS SOMETHING...?
GRRR
HE'S SO... I DUNNO... WEIRD.
ASUNA, YOU'RE SCARING HIM!
UH BOY.
NO BED SHARING! YOU GOT THAT? NONE!
YOU'LL BE ON THE COUCH, LITTLE CREEP...
ARE YOU WORRIED ABOUT YOUR CLASS?
HERE'S YOUR STUDENT LIST.
OH, THANK YOU.
YOU'LL GET USED TO HER. WE ALL DID.
NICE GIRL... FOR A PSYCHO.
NO! WELL... A FEW. GO ON IN.
DEPENDS. ARE THEY ALL LIKE ASUNA?
WOW.
...!

ざわ
YADDA
ざわ
YADDA
GOOD MORNING.
ONE, ALL RIGHT.
I WANT ONE.
DON'T YOU WANT ONE, KUGIMI?
MEAT
STOP CALLING ME THAT.
TEE HEE
HEE HEE
I'M COUNTING ON YOU.
ALL RIGHT.
HM...
NOT AGAIN...

ざわ
YADDA
YOUR HAIR!
YOU LIKE?
GOR-GEOUS...
SO...THE STUDENTS. NAMES, HOBBIES...
HM...
くす...
AND CHECK OUT THIS LENS!
GUESS SIZE DOES MATTER.
...MY STUDENTS? I'M OUT OF MY LEAGUE. OR MY MIND.
THOSE ARE...
パラッ
FWP!

GRANDAUGHTER OF SCHOOL DEAN
13. KONOKA KONOE
SECRETARY
FORTUNE-TELLING CLUB
LIBRARY CLUB
9. KASUGA MISORA
5. AKO IZUMI
NURSE'S OFFICE
SOCCER TEAM
(NON-SCHOOL ACTIVITY)
1. SAYO AIZAKA
1940~
DON'T CHANGE HER SEATING
14. HARUNA SAOTOME
MANGA CLUB
LIBRARY CLUB
10. CHACHAMARU RAKUSO
TEA CEREMONY CLUB
GO CLUB
CALL ENGINEERING (ext. A08-7796)
IN CASE OF EMERGENCY
6. AKIRA OKOCHI
SWIM TEAM
2. YUNA AKASHI
BASKETBALL TEAM
PROFESSOR AKASHI'S DAUGHTER
SETSUNA SAKURAZAKI
15 SETSUNA SAKURAZAKI
JAPANESE FENCING
11. MADOKA KUGIMIYA
CHEERLEADER
MADOKA
7. KAKIZAKI MISA
CHEERLEADER
CHORUS
3. KAZUMI ASAKU
SCHOOL NEWSPAPER
KYOTO SHINMEI STYLE
MAHORA NEWS (ext. B09-
FEI KU
16. MAKIE SASAKI
GYMNASTICS
12. FEI KU
CHINESE MARTIAL ARTS
GROUP
8. ASUNA KAGURAZAKA
ART CLUB
4. YUE AYASE
KID'S LIT CLUB
PHILOSOPHY CLUB
LIBRARY CLUB

EMERGENCY CONTACT (PRIMARY)
29. AYAKA YUKIHIRO
CLASS REPRESENTATIVE
EQUESTRIAN CLUB
FLOWER ARRANGEMENT CLUB
25. CHISAME HASEGAWA
NO CLUB ACTIVITIES
GOOD WITH COMPUTERS
21. CHIZURU NABA
ASTRONOMY CLUB
17. SAKURAKO SHIINA
LACROSS TEAM
CHEERLEADER
30. SATSUKI YOTSUBA
LUNCH REPRESENTATIVE
26. EVANGELINE A.K. MCDOWELL
GO CLUB
TEA CEREMONY CLUB
ASK HER ADVICE IF YOU'RE IN TROUBLE
22. FUKA NARUTAKI
WALKING CLUB
OLDER SISTER
FUKA TWINS
18. MANA TATSUMIYA
BIATHLON
(NON-SCHOOL ACTIVITY)
31. ZAZIE RAINYD
MAGIC
SCHOOL ACTIVITY
NODOKA MIYAZAKI
GENERAL LIBRARY
COMMITTEE MEMBER
LIBRARIAN
LIBRARY CLUB
23. FUMIKA NARUTAKI
SCHOOL DECOR CLUB
WALKING CLUB
FUMIKA
19. LINGSHEN CHAO
COOKING CLUB
CHINESE MARTIAL ARTS CLUB
ROBOTICS CLUB
CHINESE MEDICINE CLUB
BIO-ENGINEERING CLUB
QUANTUM PHYSICS CLUB (UNIVERSITY)
LINGSHEN CHAO
WOW...
HOW WILL I REMEMBER ALL THIS?!
28. NATSUMI MURAKAMI
DRAMA CLUB
24. SATOMI NAKASE
ROBOTICS CLUB (UNIVERSITY
JET PROPULSION CLUB (UNIVERSITY))
20. KAEDE NAGASE
WALKING CLUB
VERY DETERMINED
May God speed you, Negi.
Takamichi T. Takahata

GOOD LUCK WITH THEIR NAMES.
NO KIDDING.
HOW CAN I GET THEM TO TAKE ME SERIOUSLY AS A TEACHER?
I THINK I'M GONNA PUKE!! STOMACH'S ALL KNOTS.
SHE SAID THAT!? NO WAY!
YES WAY, NATSUMI!
ASUNA ALREADY HATES ME.
WORK HARD.
I WISH YOU WELL, NEGI.
ANYA... MY SISTER... I'M SCARED.
BUT IF I QUIT... I'LL LET DOWN EVERY-ONE!!
HMM
...
...
HEE HEE
TEE HEE
AND SO... IT BEGINS.
HEY.
KNOK KNOK

THWUMP
FWUP
UHMM
HELLO—
HUMP THAT NOISE...
FWOM
WOOP...
HMMM...
?!
OH MY.
I'D HEARD GIRLS WERE CLEVER.
AN ERASER ON THE HEAD ISN'T VERY ORIGINAL...
KOFF, KOFF
KOFF, KOFF
OH GREAT, OF ALL THE...
WHOA...
FOOSH
TUNK

OOF
AIEEEEE!
HUH!
HUMPH!?
FIP
FIP
PLOOSH
THUNK
WUP
WUP
WUP
HEE
HEE
HEE
HEE
HAD ENOUGH?
NEGI... GET UP.
GO AHEAD.
YOU MEAN ME?
TAKE YOUR SEATS WHILE THE PROFESSOR INTRODUCES HIMSELF.
ACTUALLY, HE IS YOUR NEW TEACHER.
KLAP KLAP
GULP
...ORIGINAL.
IT IS A KID!
WOW THAT'S...
HEY...
TMP TMP
YOU OKAY, KID?
NAH! MUST BE A MIDGET!
WE THOUGHT YOU WERE OUR NEW TEACHER.

I...
YES, WELL...
U-UH...
I LOOK FORWARD TO TEACHING YOU ALL I CAN.
MY NAME IS NEGI SPRINGFIELD. I'LL BE YOUR ENGLISH INSTRUCTOR FOR THE THIRD SEMESTER. AND I, UH...
AIEEEEEEE♡
ISN'T HE ADOR-ABLE!
...
...

THIS IS A JOKE, RIGHT?
YAP
YAP
AND AGAIN: NO.
YOUR MOM'S A WHALE?
DID YOU SAY "WHALES?"
WALES.
YES, THA– NO!
WHERE ARE YOU FROM?
DO YOU HAVE A GIRL-FRIEND?
WELL... TEN...
HOW OLD ARE YOU–!?
PRESS
WHUD
WHUD
THAT'S WHY HE'S SO SWEET.
MORE LIKE JUST DESSERTS, ACTUALLY.
THIS LITTLE CUPCAKE?
HE'S REALLY OUR TEACHER?
FWAP
FWAP
FWAP
DON'T MAKE US BEG, CUPCAKE.
AARGH
C'MON!
SAY SOME-THING SMART!
YOU'D THINK THAT, WOULDN'T YOU.
YOU MUST BE REALLY INTELLI-GENT!
BUT I'VE NO WORDS TO GET THEM OFF ME.
LANGUAGE SKILLS ARE THE ONLY THING I'M ACTUALLY GOOD AT. COLLEGE LEVEL.

...
キャーキャー
GIGGLE
YES MA'AM.
NOW BACK OFF.
キャイ
YEAH
キャイ
YEAH
HE SHOULD BE RESPECTED, NOT PAWED.
ENOUGH, LADIES. HE'S YOUR TEACHER.
GASP
OUCH, BABE.
AGUNA, WHA--?
THWUMP!
GRAB
OHHH, AGUNA'S PIGGED.
WHUD
MOI?...
WHAT "WEIRD" THING DID YOU DO TO IT?
THAT ERASER FLOATED BEFORE IT HIT YOU!
AKKKKK
IS CLASS OVER YET?
YOU HEARD SHIZUNA!
DON'T MAKE HIM CRY FOR MOMMY!
BAM BAM
AW, AGUNA, C'MON!
SAVE YOUR FANCY GREEK WORDS!
WHOAA-AAAAAA!!! EVERYBODY JUST WHOA!

EASE UP THE STIRRUPS BEFORE YOU BUST OUR LITTLE BRONCO.
JUST REIN IT IN, PEOPLE.
YOU WANT TO EMBARRASS YOURSELF?
DO IT ON YOUR OWN TIME. BUT DON'T DRAG THIS CLASS DOWN WITH YOU.
PUT HIM DOWN, ASUNA-SAN.
SAVE YOUR YAKKING, AYAKA.
TUG
HMPH
THANKS... AYAKA.
UH...
THAT MAKES HIM MORE QUALIFIED THAN ANYONE HERE...
...ESPECIALLY YOU. NOW PLEASE, PROFESSOR... CONTINUE YOUR REMARKS.
I HEAR NEGI-SENSEI IS AN OXFORD-EDUCATED GENIUS.

BEING A "GOODY-GOODY" COMES NATURAL TO ME, THAT'S ALL.
IT'S NO ACT.
AYAKA-SAN'S GOT HER CLASS REP GOODY-GOODY ACT DOWN PAT.
SAY... WHAT?
...WHAT'S SO NATURAL ABOUT BEING INTO LITTLE BOYS?!
HEH. HERE I THOUGHT...
URK
WONK
YAHH
YAHH
SENIOR CITIZENS?!
TAKAHATA-SENSEI'S ANCIENT! HE'S, LIKE, THIRTY!
YOU SHUT UP ABOUT HIM RIGHT NOW!
SOMEONE WHO'S INTO SENIOR CITIZENS DOESN'T GET TO—
WHOA
YE-YES MA'AM.
ALL RIGHT EVERYONE, ENOUGH FUN. EDUCATION AWAITS YOU.
NEGI-SENSEI? THEY'RE ALL YOURS.
KLAP
SHEESH.
"FUN?"
TWENTY ON AYAKA!!
SETTLE DOWN!
GO ASUNA!
LADIES!
OHHH, THIS IS NOT GOING WELL. SHIZUNA WILL WRITE ME UP... I'LL BE FIRED♪ I....

HAVE TO FOCUS ON NOT LETTING MY SISTER, ANYA, DOWN...
THINK... THINK...
...
HMM...
HMMMM
MMBL...
MMBL...
TEE HEE
A LITTLE HELP, PLEASE?
LITTLE IS RIGHT!
HEEE
TEE HEE
UH...
NUTS.
HEE HEE
ALL RIGHT, LADIES. TURN TO PAGE 128 IN...
UNH...
REACH REACH
YES, THANK YOU, AYAKA.
WHEW
PERHAPS THIS FOOT-STOOL, SIR?
HA...
TEE HEE HEE

NOW WE CAN ALL SEE WHAT YOU WRITE.
HA HA HA
THAT WAS MY PLAN...
...YEAH.
...
HE'S SO CUTE
HE CAN FOOL THE OTHERS, BUT NOT ME.
ONCE I PROVE HE'S A WEIRDO...
...HE'S TOAST.
ZWING
C'MON. FLOAT IT, LIKE THE ERASER.
?
?
OW!!
TONK
THUNK
OW.
OWW!!
THUNK
I'M TRYING TO.
ASUNA! KNOCK IT OFF!
ZWING
ZWING

PROBLEM, SIR?
WELL, EITHER YOU PEOPLE HAVE REALLY HARD MOSQUITOS...
SHE'S CHUCKING ROCKS.
YOU MEAN ASUNA-SAN?
KEEP AN EYE ON HER.
びくんっ
URK
WHY IS SHE—?
GIRL'S GOT MORE ISSUES THAN THE JAPAN TIMES. DROPPED ON THE HEAD AS A BABY...
...REPEATEDLY. PLUS, SHE WATCHES A LOT OF TV. ALL THAT SEX, VIOLENCE...
MMBL
MMBL
ボソ
ボソ
MMBL
MMBL
OH! WELL, UH...
SAY NO MORE.
THUMP
THUMP
ドタ
バタ
ARRGH
THUD
ガタン
TUNK
ARGH
OH DARN... CLASS IS OVER...
BONG
BONG...
キーン
コーン
カーン
アハハハ
HA HA HA
HMM. I USED ALL MY ROCKS AND HE DIDN'T STOP A SINGLE ONE.
DON'T WORRY. YOU CAN GET MORE ROCKS... FROM YOUR HEAD.

HOW WENT YOUR FIRST CLASS, NEGI-SENSEI?
FINE, WHATEVER.
C'MON! I GOTTA PICK SOMETHING UP.
ZHOOP
MMM HMMM.
NEGI-SENSEI, THANKS AGAIN FOR TEACHING US! I JUST LOVE THIS GUY, TAKAHATA-SENSEI.
RUBB
RUBB
SIIIIGH
OH, THANKS!
HE-HELLO, TAKAHATA-SENSEI!
NOT... EXACTLY AS I'D HOPED, TAKAMICHI. IT WAS–
FSSH
SOOO... GOT A YEN FOR TAKAMICHI, HUH?
HMMM...
PAT
PAT
TAKA-HATA-SENSEI. ♥
JUST HAPPY TO BE NO-TICED...
IT'S NICE TO KNOW YOU'RE THERE PROVIDING SUPPORT FOR HIM, ASUNA. I APPRECIATE IT.
TMP
...NEXT TIME IT'LL BE BRICKS, NOT ROCKS.
OH, FORGET IT. BUT IF YOU SAY ONE WORD TO HIM ABOUT IT...
URK
YUKK
IT'S SO UNFAIR. YOU'RE HIS PAL, AND I'M...
OH, ZIP IT.
ASUNA! OVER HERE!
DON'T LET HER GET TO YOU.
GIGGLE

キーン BONG コーン BONG カーン... BONG...
MAN, I THOUGHT THE DAY WOULD NEVER END.
"SH'RIGHT" INDEED.
SH'RIGHT.
THAT "KID" IS THE NEW TEACHER!
HEY, KID! GET OUR BALL, WOULD YOU?
WONDER WHAT HER DEAL IS.
AND THAT ASUNA! WHAT A NIGHT-MARE!
LEAST-WAYS I HOPE SO.
THE ONLY UPSIDE IS TOMORROW CAN'T BE WORSE.
CHECK THE PLANNER...
SHE'S MADE LIFE HELL FOR ME.
SHE'D LIKELY SMOTHER ME IN MY SLEEP.
HOW AM I SUPPOSED TO BUNK AT HER PLACE?
MAHORA NEWS (02)-809-3780
FEI KU
CHINESE MARTIAL ARTS GROUP
8. ASUNA KAGURAZAKA
ART CLUB
4. YUE AYASE
ASUNA KAGURAZAKA. "ART CLUB." NOT MUCH HERE.

TEE HEE
12. FEI KU
BOO!
8. ASUNA KAGURAZAKA
FWIK
FWIK
HMP
POO
POO
THERE. RETURNED THE FAVOR.
FWIM FWAM
HUFF
HUFF
SHE LOOKS TOO LOADED DOWN. SHE COULD—
NOW THAT'S...
STUDENT NUMBER 27, NODOKA MIYAZAKI-SAN...

AHHHH !!
くきっ
KRIK
SNAK
I KNEW IT!
...HM?
WHAT'S THE BRAT DO-?
TP
TP
FWOOSH
AIEEEE!

ふわりっ
WOOOOMF
GOTCHA!!
THUNK

YOU ALL RIGHT, NODOKA-SAN...? YOU ALMOST HIT THE GROUND PRETTY—
UNNNEFF!
ぐばきゅっ
SQUISSH
ズリィィィ
WUUUNK

YOU...
YOU'RE...
UR...
NE-
NEGI ...?
GRAAAB
FWOOSH
WHUP
HEY...
RUN
RUN
RUN
RUN
...
WELL... HEH...
GOTTA GO...

YOU MADE HER FLOAT! I SAW IT!
TH-THAT'S RIDICU-
FLOAT LONG ENOUGH TO "CATCH" HER! HOW?!
URGH
YOU'RE SOME KIND OF PSYCHIC! OR ALIEN?
FWISH FWISH
I-I'M A MAGICIAN, OKAY?...
EITHER WAY, YOU'RE WEIRD!
HEY...
YOU'RE WHY MY DRESS BLEW OFF THIS MORNING!
HOW DARE YOU—!
AIEE
IT WAS AN ACCIDENT!
I DIDN'T MEAN FOR...! PLEASE DON'T TELL ANYONE.
ANYONE? I'M TELLING EVERYONE!
THEN I'VE NO CHOICE.
URK
NO CHOICE BUT, UH, WHAT?
I'LL HAVE TO ERASE YOUR MEMORY!
FWOOSH!
WHAT !?

ANCIENT BEINGS, FAR AND NEAR, MAKE HER MEMORY–
ゴゴゴゴゴゴ!!
RRRRRRR!!
NOW HOLD ON!
LET'S TALK THIS–
–DISAPPEAR !!!
AIEE
!?
パーン
ウウウ
NO-
UH OH.

OH...
FSH
SO, NEGI, MAKING FRIENDS, I SEE.
OKAY. THAT'S NOT RIGHT.
UNHHH
HM...
UR-URGH
DA DOOM
N-
AIEE
I- I'M SO SORRY.
アホ KAHH
アホ KAHH
DEATH
DESPAIR
NOOOOOOO

STILL THERE?! MY HUMILIATION WILL BE SEARED INTO MY BRAIN UNTIL I DIE!
MEMORY STILL THERE, HUH?
I GUESS THE ANCIENT BEINGS DON'T SPEAK JAPANESE.
AIEEEE
わーん
YOU SHOULD WANT TO LIVE!
DON'T SAY THAT!
WHICH, HOPEFULLY, WILL BE JUST ABOUT ANY TIME NOW!
TUMP
ドンドンドン
TUMP
TUMP
WHY ARE YOU HERE, ANYWAY?!
SNIFFL SNIFFL
I DO! LONG ENOUGH TO SEE YOU DIE FIRST!
ポロ
FLIP
ポロ
AIEEE
GRAAB
I'M IN TRAINING...
...TO BE A "MAGISTER MAGI"...

NOW WE LIVE IN MORE "RATIONAL" TIMES, SO WE'RE MORE SECRETIVE.
ITS MOST APPARENT MANIFESTATION IS IN THE UNITED NATIONS NGO...
A MAGISTER MAGI IS LIKE A GUARDIAN ANGEL, HELPING PEOPLE AND THE WORLD. IN ANCIENT TIMES, WE DID SO OPENLY.
IT'S A SORCEROUS RANK...
A WHAT NOW?

C'MON... GIMME A BREAK...
MAYBE GET TURNED INTO A HAMSTER.
I... I'D BE RECALLED... LOSE MY LICENSE, ...
AIEEE
あうううっ

UH HUH. AND IF EVERYONE KNEW ABOUT YOUR MAGIC?
RIGHT NOW I'VE GOT A KIND OF TEMPORARY LICENSE.

A HAMSTER, HUH.
ゴゴ... GRR...
A BREAK? SURE. WHICH ARM?

MAYBE... IF YOU REALLY WANT TO MAKE UP FOR–
SOUNDS HUMILIATING. AND RIGHT NOW, I SURE CAN RELATE TO WHAT IT'S LIKE BEING HUMILIATED.
DOOOM
どおん
くすっ... SNIFF...
DEFINITELY!
I DO!

WHAT OTHER KIND OF MAGIC DO YOU DO?
DIFFERENT STUFF. MOSTLY SIMPLE. I'M, Y'KNOW, STILL LEARNING.
IF NOT, I SWEAR I'LL EXPOSE YOU IN A WHOLE DIFFERENT WAY THAN YOU DID ME.
I'LL GET RIGHT ON IT.
I SAID I'M ON IT.
YOU HAVE TO MAKE IT SO I'M NOT "HEART-BROKEN." SO TAKAHATA-SENSEI DOESN'T THINK I'M A...
...WHATEVER HE THINKS I AM.

HAVE MORE MONEY.
FWAP
ASUNA, BE MINE!
NUTS! OKAY—A TREE THAT GROWS MONEY, THEN! I'LL BUY HIS LOVE!
DUNNO THAT ONE EITHER.

OH, TAKAHATA-SENSEI!
ASUNA, BE MINE!
A LOVE POTION! I COULD GIVE IT TO—
SORRY, NO...
PLISH

MY GRADES WOULD AGREE WITH YOU. OH... I CAN READ MINDS...
BOY, YOU'RE NOT MUCH OF A MAGICIAN, ARE YOU.

MMBL MMBL
...FIND OUT HIS TRUE FEELINGS FOR ME.
FANTASTIC! YOU CAN READ TAKAHATA-SENSEI'S MIND...

ZHOOP
LET'S GET RIGHT TO IT!
I JUST HAVE TO GRAB SOME STUFF FROM MY...

NOW YOU TELL ME ?!?!
URK

パーパーパーパーパーパーパーパー!!
POPP
POPP
POPPOOM
WELCOME
NEGI-SENSEI!!
HUH...
THE GUEST OF HONOR SITS IN THE MIDDLE.
THANKS, GIRLS!
YADDA
YADDA
ワイワイ
ワー
HURRAH
HERE'RE THE PARTY SNACKS.
いえー
YEAHH
UH... OKAY...
...ROOM. TERRIFIC. A SURPRISE WELCOMING PARTY.

NO, JUST MY CLOTHES. AGAIN. DON'T ASK.
I THOUGHT YOU LOST YOUR WAY...
アハハ
HA HA HA
YADDA YADDA
YOUR JAPANESE IS SO GOOD!!
YOU'RE SO CUTE.
HAVE THESE SPECIAL MEAT BUNS!

OH...
NUMBER 27, NODOKA MIYAZAKI-SAN, THE LIBRARIAN.
NEGI-SENSEI...
UMM...
WHAT A WELCOMING PARTY. I GUESS I WORRIED FOR NOTHING.
ワイワイ

...
I'D'VE BROKEN MY NECK IF NOT FOR YOU. I WANTED TO THANK YOU...

...
ガタッ
THUMP
アハハハ
HA HA HA
DRY UP, KAKIZAKI!
おお
WOW
UH, THANKS.
HERE'S DISCOUNT COUPONS FROM THE SCHOOL BOOKSTORE. IT'S NOT MUCH, BUT...
COUPONS! FOR NODOKA, THAT'S FIRST BASE.
ワイワイ!?

AT LEAST I KEEP MINE COVERED UP!
SHE SEES A BOY AND TROTS OUT HER BUST...
どぎゃーん
ZING
WOW! SHE'S GIVING HIM A BUST!
AND THIS IS FROM ME, TO REMEMBER THE DAY.
Negi Springfield
WHAT ELSE IS NEW?
TRUE ENOUGH, TAKAMACHI. HELLO SHIZUNA-SENSEI.
ギャーギャー
AIEE AIEEE
GO GO
I'M BETTING ¥100 ON AYAKA.
CAT FIGHT!
¥200 ON ASUNA!
HELLO NEGI. YOUR DAY FINALLY IMPROVING?
KOFF
ゴスッ
THUNK
TAKAHATA-SENSEI!?
G-GOT IT.
OKAY, THIS IS IT. IF YOU SCREW THIS UP, GO BUY YOURSELF A HAMSTER WHEEL. GET IT?
ぐぎぎ
GOOD!!
GET IT?

HUH?
HEY, TAKAMICHI.
ヒタリ
FIP...
HA HA/ WELL, JUST KEEP ON WORKING ON IT, YOU'LL BE FINE.
IT DIDN'T GO SO WELL...
YES, OF COURSE, A TOAST.
ワイワイ
YAP YAP
A TOAST TO NEGI-SENSEI
RIGHT.
AND BE SUBTLE/
?
みょみょみょ
VWEEWEEP
WHAT DO YOU THINK OF ASUNA-SAN?
VWOOP
KRRSH
THAT'S SUBTLE?!?
ぐしゃ
SQUIEL
OF ALL THE-!
あわわわ
ARRGH
A BIT SHORT TEMPERED, BUT OTHERWISE A GOOD KID.
WE-WELL... SHE'S A HARD WORKER. CHEERFUL, ENERGETIC...
?
タタタ
TP TP TP
HMMM

SWOOSH
HE'S THINKING YOU DON'T WEAR PANTIES.
O-OKAY...
FIND OUT SOMETHING MORE!
?
ARRGH!
WELL, THAT'S PERFECT!
?
TP TP TP...
TP TP TP...
...
ASUNA!
TMP
ZHOOP
KRRSH
HE'S THINKING YOU WEAR BEAR PANTIES.

WA-WAIT, ASUNA-SAN!
LEAVE ME ALONE!
LOOK, I KINDA LIED! THERE IS A LOVE POTION!
IT JUST TAKES FOUR MONTHS TO PREPARE, THAT'S ALL!
GO AWAY!
I JUST WANT TO HELP, THAT'S ALL.
I DON'T CARE ABOUT THAT RIGHT NOW. I JUST...
SO BUZZ OFF.
I WON'T TELL YOUR STUPID SECRET, OKAY?
HUH.
I CAN'T REMEMBER THE LAST TIME...
...SOMEONE JUST WANTED TO HELP ME.
THIS LOVE POTION... IS IT GUARANTEED?
...
...
NO...
IT'S PRETTY UNRELIABLE.
SORCERY ISN'T REALLY SUPPOSED TO BE USED FOR THAT.
MY GRANDFATHER SAID...

...
ドキ
TUMP!
OUR MAGIC IS NOT ABSOLUTE.
TRUE MAGIC RESULTS FROM COURAGE OF THE HEART.

HEY...!
TP
TP
TP
FWIP
YOUR GRAND-FATHER WAS A DOPE.
...
SQUEEK...
FWIP...
OKAY...
I'LL BE MORE COURAGEOUS.

YOU'LL BE MY GUINEA PIG.
BUT I NEED TO USE YOU.
OH...
NOT LITERALLY. I NEED TO PRACTICE TELLING HIM HOW I FEEL.
YOUR ...?
トン TUMP
...
...
WELL...
UH...
するっ.. FWIP
...
BRRING..
UH...
HMMM...
SO YOU PRETEND YOU'RE TAKAHATA-SENSEI.
O-OKAY.

I LOVE YOU.

ぴキぃ...
TWLIMP...
I LOVE YOU...
...TEACHER.

OH...
UH NO... BUT...
SHE LOOKS LIKE MY SISTER WITH HER HAIR DOWN.
I'VE LOVED YOU FOR SO LONG...
I HOPE YOU'RE NOT OFFENDED.
I KNEW I'M NOT GOOD ENOUGH...
FWIP
HEY!
YOU'RE GOOD ENOUGH!
TUGG
TWUMP
...YOU THINK SO...?
TUNK
HEY
...!
...
U-UH...
TWUMP TWUMP TWUMP
TWUMP TWUMP TWUMP
OH, TEACHER...
...I'VE... I'VE...
HUHP
...
TWUMP TWUMP
TWUMP TWUMP TWUMP
...

WAITED SO LONG FOR THIS...!
ドキドキ
TWUMP TWUMP
ドキ
TWUMP
ドキ...
TWUMP...

むにっ
BWEEEM

UNGH...
HUH...

SUCKER!
HA...
HA HA HA

アハハ
HA HA
ぽっぺたぷにぷにぃ
RUBBER CHEEK'S
ぽらぽら
CHECK IT OUT
YOU WANNA KIIIIS'S ME. YOU WANNA MAAAAKE OUT...

YOUR CHEEK'S ARE FLUSHED. YOU GET PRETTY WORKED UP FOR A KID.
うりうりっ
HUHH ARGH
YOU REALLY THOUGHT I'D KISS YOUR RUNTY FACE?!
DO NOT!
ばばたた
FIP FAP
じたじた
FIP FAP

WEEM
UNGH...
UH...

パシャ
SNAPP
パシャ
SNAPP
パシャ
SNAPP
HUH...

WOWEE!
A-ASUNA-SAN...
AHEM
BRR
UH...
HEY...
WHAT!?
YEAHH
AND YOU, "PROFESSOR!" CONDUCT UNBECOMING A FACULTY MEMBER!
AT LEAST I DO THINK! UNLIKE SOME I KNOW!
IT'S NOT WHAT YOU THINK.
NOW WHO'S THE ONE INTO CRADLE-ROBBING, HUH?
I WAS JUST... JUST-!
ズギャ
AYAHHH
WING
FWING
LO-LO-
YAHH
BUT...
BUT... BUT...
INTOLERABLE, PROFESSOR!
THIS HAS TO BE REPORTED!

WOOH WOOH
WOO HOO! FAST WORKER!
IS THAT WHAT HE WANTS?
YOU WANT TO MAKE EVERYBODY NAKED?!?
KNOCK IT OFF!
LOSE YOUR MEMOR--!!
SHUDDUP, THE LOT OF YOU!

YOU HAD IT COMING.
CONSIDERING IT'S ALL YOUR FAULT...
THOUGH I WOULDN'T BLAME THEM.
OH, STOP SNIVELING. NO ONE'S REPORTING YOU.

WHO'D TAKE YOU SERIOUSLY AS TEACHER?
...BUT YOU'RE STILL A BRAT.
YOU MIGHT BE SOME HOTSHOT MAGICIAN...
YOU KNOW I'M RIGHT.
UR...

...

MAYBE ¿I SHOULD GIVE UP NOW?
URGH... SHE'S RIGHT. I'M THE ONE WHO'S NOT GOOD ENOUGH.

G-
GO WHERE?
COME ON, LET'S GO.
ASUNA-
...I LIKED THAT YOU TRIED TO HELP.
BE-SIDES...
FIP FIP FIP
HUH...
NOW I'M SAYING DIFFERENT.
BUT YOU SAID-
HOME, DUMB-ASS. CAN'T LEAVE YOU IN THE STREET.
...IN THE END.
YOU MIGHT MAKE A HALFWAY DECENT TEACHER...
THANK YOU!
Y' THINK!? WOW!
ME ...?
FWIK FWIK
キュ キュ...
...
FWIP
HAH

THIS MIGHT ACTUALLY ALL TURN OUT OKAY.
ANYA...
MY SISTER...
ACTUALLY A GOOD PERSON
GURAZAKA
4. YU
AND A GOOD MAGICIAN AT THAT.
I MIGHT BE A GOOD TEACHER...
YO! LEAD-FOOT! MOVE!
YES! I'M COMING!
I...
UH... AH...
AH CHOO!
AIEEEE
AIEE... NEGI!!
I'M SO SORRY.

FSSHH...
キアアア
TAKAHATA-SENSEI... UM...
I MADE SOME DELICIOUS TEA.
I WAS WONDERING IF YOU'D LIKE SOME.
LET ME GUESS: LOVE POTION, RIGHT?
YOU DON'T NEED THIS.
すっ
FSH...
ホレ
LOVE
I...
I DON'T, SIR?
WHA-T !?
I'VE ALWAYS LOVED YOU!
はっはっ
はっは
HA
HM...
OH...
ぐぐ
TUGG...
ASUNA-KUN...
TA-TAKAHATA-SENSEI...

2ND PERIOD: PANIC IN THE LIBRARY!?

AIEEEEEEEE
UMM...
SIS...
HE-
HMM...
...!?
HEY...
...WHAT ARE YOU DOING IN MY BED!?
WHOA !!!
ZZZ

A-ASUNA-SAN!?
I-I-I'M SO SORRY. I USED TO SLEEP IN THE SAME ROOM AS MY SISTER AND I JUST...
WHAT DO I HAVE TO DO...
...TIE YOU TO THE SOFA?!
NAH. KNOWING YOU, YOU'D LIKE THAT!
OH NO!! IT'S 5 AM! GOTTA MOVE!
WHUD
WHUD
CHUD
WHERE'S ASUNA-SAN GOING?
HMMM, HER JOB.
I'LL MAKE EGGS FOR BREAKFAST, NEGI-KUN.
pooh
YOU WANT YOUR'S SCRAMBLED OR SUNNY SIDE UP?
UH...
どうも
THANKS
SUNNY SIDE UP, I GUESS.
HMM
GOT IT.
...
THAT'S RIGHT.

I THINK ASUNA-SAN, KONOKA-SAN AND I ARE REALLY BONDING.
MY STAYING HERE WAS GOOD FOR ALL OF US.
FOOD'S ON!
CHIRP
CHIRP
NEGI, YOU JERK!
GIMME A BREAK, WOULD YOU?
WOULD IT HAVE KILLED YOU TO PUT THE TOILET SEAT DOWN?!
BONG
BONG...
I DIDN'T NEED MORE DELAYS, THANKS!
YOU GUYS NEED TO GET ALONG.
WHUD
WHUD
WHUD

MMBL
YOU... YOU'RE BLUFFING. YOU WOULDN'T–
I'M THE ONLY ONE WHO KNOWS YOU'RE A MAGICIAN.
WHUD
LET'S NOT FORGET SOME-THING.
YE-YES!?
TUGG
WHUD
OKAY, OKAY, I BELIEVE YOU!
I IMAGINE YOU'LL BE BURNED AT THE STAKE. YO! EVERYBODY! MAGICIAN, RIGHT OVER HERE!
TUGG...
TA-KAHATA-SENSEI...
ASUNA-KUN...
HMMM ...?
TWUMP...
SO, UHM...ARE YOU STILL INTERESTED IN THAT LOVE POTION I MENTIONED YESTERDAY?
?
DEAL.
SO NO MORE CLOTHES YANKING. GOT IT?
...
ARGH
WHUMP
WHAT'S WITH THE MIXED SIGNALS, HUH?!

YOU'RE THE ONE WHO SAID COURAGE IS THE TRUEST FORM OF MAGIC.
I'LL DO THIS ON MY OWN, THANKS.
OH...
WELL...GOOD FOR HER! MAYBE I ACTUALLY TAUGHT HER SOMETHING!
GOOD GOING, ASUNA-SAN.
YADDA YADDA
ワイ ワイ..
AND IF SHE CAN FIND COURAGE... FACE DIFFICULTIES...
HM?
THEN I BET I CAN DO THE SAME THING.
...SO I CAN BECOME A MAGISTER MAGI LIKE MY GRANDFATHER.
HMMM.
STUPID OUT-OF-REACH LOCKER.
すっ
FSH...
カタン
LINK...

GOOD MORNING, NEGI-SENSEI.
TUK...
I'LL WALK YOU TO OUR CLASS-ROOM.
TH-THANK YOU.
OH...
DAY DUTY NOTE No.17
2ND YEAR CLASS A
JUNIOR HIGH
YOU'RE... AYAKA YUKIHIRO, RIGHT? CLASS REP?
GETTING OUR NAMES DOWN QUICKLY, I SEE. DID YOU SLEEP WELL?
YES, THANK'S.
ZHOOP
ガラッ
FWEE...
THUP
OH...
GOOD MORNING.
GO-GOOD MORNING.
TEACHER APPROACHES!
STAND!
ガタ
ガタン...
CHUD
CHUD...
UGH.

HI...
OH...
FWICH
ATTENNNN-SHUN!
FIP
BOW.
GOOD MORNING, SIR.
I-I KNOW, ASUNA-SAN.
RELAAAAAX.
BE SEAT-ED—
...MORN-ING.
GOOD...
CHUD
CHUD

PICKING UP FROM YESTERDAY...
...LET'S TURN TO PAGE 128 IN OUR TEXTS.
NEO HORIZON

WHO CAN TRANSLATE THIS PASSAGE INTO JAPANESE? ANYONE?
ANYONE?
TOK TOK
コッ コッ
NEO HORIZON

"The fall of Jason the flower. Spring came. Jason the flower was born on a branch of a tall tree. Hundreds of flowers were born on the tree. They were all friends."
SO FAR, SO GOOD. THIRTY SECONDS AND NO RIOTS. A RECORD.
TOK TOK
コッ コッ

FSSH...

FSH...
NEO HORIZON

...
UNGGGH...
WIRRL
WIRRL
BRRR
BRRR
...

BECAUSE WHY? WHY NOT START WITH SOMEBODY ELSE?!?
BE-BE-CAUSE...
WH-WHY ME!?
CHUD
ASUNA-SAN!
NEO HORIZON
WELL YOU'RE WRONG!
...TO SHOW OFF YOUR KNOWLEDGE FOR YOUR CLASS-MATES.
"OPPORTU-NITY?!"
BECAUSE I THOUGHT YOU'D LIKE THE OPPORTUNITY–
UMM...
FINE, I'LL TRANSLATE IT, OKAY?
THAT'S NOT–
HA HA ホホ
SO ASUNA, YOU ADMIT YOU DON'T GET THIS PASSAGE.
I'LL DO IT FOR YOU...
...
THAT IS... BONES... WERE... THE TREES...
LET'S SEE... THEY ATE BRUNCH ON THE TALL TREE... AND THEN THERE WERE BONES... HUNDRED'S OF THEM?
JASON WAS...ON THE FLOWER... AND FELL. THEN SPRING CAME? JASON AND THE FLOWER.

TEE HEE
HA HA
NOT GOOD-?!
HA HA HA
TEE HEE
OKAY... NOT BAD. NOT GOOD, BUT-
NEO HORIZON
HA HA HA
FOOSH
...THAT RAINBOW BRIDGE WAS A CARD GAME.
SHE'S SO DUMB SHE THOUGHT...
OR SCIENCE OR HISTORY.
OR LITERATURE...
SHE'S NOT MUCH BETTER AT MATH.
NO ...!
TUGG
YOU TRIED TO EMBARRASS ME, DIDN'T YOU!
AH CHOO!!
WAIT!
DON'T-!
UH OH ...!?
AH...
AH...
I... UH...
FSH
URRR

AIEEEE
FWOOOOSH
AIEEE
HEY!
GOOD MOVE, ASUNA-SAN...
...WITH YOUR GRADES, A CAREER AS A STRIPPER IS YOUR BEST BET.
HMMMM...
BOY! DRAFTY IN HERE!
HA HA HA HA
HA HA HA
...TO KILL YOU!!
I'M GOING...
WHUM
BONG
BONG
BONG
AIEEE...

I THOUGHT I WAS HELPING ASUNA-SAN...
-S-I-G-H-
SHE JUST GLARED AT ME FOR THE REST OF THE CLASS.
BUT I JUST EMBARRASSED HER AGAIN.
YES!?
HM...
UM, NEGI-SENSEI...
RIGHT NAME, BUT NOT MY QUESTION. IT'S HERS.
SURE. WHAT'S YOUR QUESTION... HARUNA-SAN, RIGHT?
OH. OKAY.
ゴソ ゴソ
FP FP
UMM UMM...
おず おず...
YES. I...
NO... DOKA?
CAN WE ASK YOU ABOUT TODAY'S LESSON?

I TOLD YOU!
I LIKE YOUR NEW HAIRDO. LOOKS NICE.
SHE FINALLY GOT IT OUT OF HER FACE.
IT'S SUCH A CUTE DO!
I TOLD YOU HE'D NOTICE IT!
HEY...
HUH...
OKAY. THAT WAS STRANGE.
HUH... OH...
OH, NODOKA!
GOMEN NASAI, SENSEI.
NEGI-
カアアッ
FOOSH
HEY, NODOKA-SAN!!
TMP
HMP
SHLIP...
MAN, WHAT DO I DO ABOUT-?
HAHHH キシャ
BUT ASUNA-SAN... SHE'S STRANGER THAN MOST.
I GUESS THEY ALL ARE IN DIFFERENT WAYS.

...THAT TUBE OF "MAGIC ESSENCE" PILLS GRANDFATHER GAVE ME...!!
TH-THIS IS...!?
ALL RIGHT THEN!
ANYA MUST HAVE PACKED IT IN MY BAG FOR ME.
I COULD MAYBE MAKE A LOVE POTION WITH THIS!!
...AND I CAN'T BLAME HER.
RIGHT NOW SHE DOESN'T TRUST ME...
...BETTER NOT TELL ASUNA YET.
UM...
I...
I DID IT.
KOFF
KOFF
Potion Amoris!!
age nascatur
FOOM
RAS TER MA SKIL
GLUG
GL
MAKISTEL

JUNIOR HIGH 2ND YEAR CLASS A
THEN SHE'LL FORGIVE ME!
IT'S GONNA WORK! I KNOW IT! ONCE SHE DRINKS THIS, TAKAMICHI WON'T BE ABLE TO RESIST HER!
NEGI LOOKS EXCITED!
WONDER WHY?
I'LL SEE HERE
ZHOOP
ASUNA-SAN! ASUNA-SAN!
OH, WHAT LUCK. I WAS TIRED OF BEING DRESSED.
DID WHAT?
I MADE IT!
LOVE POTION. THE LOVE POTION.
THUP
FIP
TMP
WHAT HAPPENED TO "FOUR MONTHS."
C'MON! I'M SURE IT WORKS!
WHAT DO YOU WANT?
HMM!
I DID IT!
I DID IT!
STOMP
STOMP
STOMP
I FOUND A SHORT CUT! TRY IT!

GLUGG
YOU TRY IT, MR. WIZARD!
TUGG
HUMMPH
GULPP
HAK
KOFF
KOFF
...
GLUG
GLUG
AND MAYBE YOU'LL GET YOUR CLOTHES TORN OFF THIS TIME...
BECAUSE YOU SUCK AT MAGIC.
NO, IT SHOULDN'T. Y'KNOW WHY?
THAT'S STRANGE. IT SHOULD WORK...
HUH. FIGURES.
...THE MORE ADORABLE YOU LOOK.
...THE LONGER I STARE AT YOU...
NEGI-KUN...
SORRY. I GUESS MAGIC'S LIKE LOVE: NO SHORT-CUTS.
HMF.

KONOKA-SAN?
HMMMM
KONOKA! GET A GRIP!
AND I DON'T MEAN ON HIM!
CHUD

AS CLASS REP,
GRAB
I WILL NOT TOLERATE THIS...
THIS...
GRAB
HUH...
...THIS BOUQUET OF FLOWERS GOING TO ANYONE BUT YOU, NEGI-SENSEI!
FWICH
?!

FWOOSH
THIS OUTFIT I MADE FOR MY KID BROTHER WOULD FIT YOU!
I BAKED THIS DESSERT FOR YOU IN COOKING CLASS!
HUH...
LET'S GET HIS NEW CLOTHES ON HIM... AND THESE OFF!
SAY AH!
C'MON!
KNOCK IT OFF!
HUH. GUESS IT DOES WORK AT THAT.

ASUNA-SAN! HE-L-L-PPP!
WHUD
WHUD
WHUD
WHUD
WHL
NEGI-SENSEI! COME BACK!

THOK
HUH
SNAP OUT OF IT, AYAKA!

UNGH
A-ASUNA! WHERE'D HE GO?!

HUH...
FWIP
FWIP
YOU'RE KIDDING, RIGHT?

WE LOVE YOU, NEGI-SENSEI!
WHUD
WHUD
WHUD
WHUD
AIEEEEE

HUH
TUGG
OKAY. THIS WAY, SIR.

HIDING NOW! EXPLAINING LATER!
WHUD
WHUD
FROM WHO, SIR?

NODOKA-SAN! HIDE ME!
WHUD
WHUD
HEY!

ガチャリ!
CHAK...
YOU'RE A LIFESAVER, NODOKA-SAN.
NO PROBLEM.
I LOCKED IT SO YOU SHOULD BE SAFE FOR...
ハア ハア...
HUF HUF...
ふぅ
PHOO
...NOW?
BABUMP-BABUMP
URK
WOW-♥
THE SCHOOL WAS FOUNDED BY A EUROPEAN A LONG TIME AGO.
PLENTY OF TIME TO AMASS A COLLECTION.
BUT THE COLLEGE LIBRARY HAS MILLIONS MORE.
WOW-
THIS LIBRARY'S HUGE!
NEVER SEEN SO MANY BOOKS!
OH, UH... YES.
SO YOU'RE THE LIBRARY EXPERT, HUH?
OH... NO...

WH-WHAT'S WRONG?
じ
HMMMM
...
スススッ...
FSSSH...
スススッ...
FSSSH...
ASUNA-SAN-!
ASU-!
OH, NEGI-SENSEI...
NEGI-SENSEI
THIS TIME IT'S MY FAULT...
STUPID KID WAS JUST TRYING TO HELP ME.
WHUD
WHUD
WHUD
NEGI! OKAY! I'M READY TO HELP YOU NOW!
STOP!
TUNK
THAT SOUNDED LIKE BOOK-STORE GIRL'S VOICE!
TP

AGEEEE
AIEEE
OH...
THUNK
A-ARE YOU ALL RIGHT, NODOKA-SAN?
ゴッ
OUCH
OH...
THUD
THUD
THUD
WHEEEE!
ARGH
ずるっ
SHLIP
WHAT...
OH, WATCH OUT!
ババッ
FIP
NO...
IT'S LOCKED?!?
ガチャ
CHAK
NOW WHAT?!
ガチャ
CHAK

I'VE NEVER BEEN...
...WITH A MAN BEFORE.
WELL, ME NEITHER.
WHY'D I MAKE THAT DUMB POTION?
OH... BROTHER.
...NEGI...
OH...
HMMM
YOU'LL HATE YOUR-SELF/ OR ME/
OR... OR BOTH/
WHEN YOU RECOVER YOUR SENSES...
FMM...
NO-DOKA/ STOP/
FM...
UH
I... I SUPPOSE...
YOU'RE RIGHT.

SHOOOM...
...
WAIT. NO. YOU'RE WRONG.
I COULD NEVER HATE YOU.
WHIRL
FOCUS CHI. AND... Hiii!
YAAAAAH!!!
WAK
AIEEE
THUD
ARGH
KRAKK
BOY, THERE'S GRATITUDE!
I- I'M SORRY!
URRR
GEEEZ.
ASUNA-SAN! YOU COULD'A KILLED SOMEBODY!

KRICH...
"MAGISTER MAGI" NEGI...
MORE LIKE "MASTER INGRATE."
Y-YOU'RE RIGHT. THANKS. AND, HEY... NICE KICK.
HUH...
WHAT WERE WE DOING ...?
アホ— アホッ KAHH KAHH
WHAT'S TOMORROW, NEGI-SENSEI? A PLAGUE?
ANOTHER DAY, ANOTHER FIASCO.
THANKS FOR SAVING ME, ASUNA-SAN.
んあ～ YAHHN

YEAH. SURE YOU DID.
I DIDN'T. I SAVED NODOKA FROM HUMILIATING HERSELF.

WUMP
STOP CAUSING TROUBLE! GET IT?
GOT IT!

VERY CUTE
27. NODOKA MIYAZAKI

ACTUALLY GOOD FOR SOMEONE!
8. ASUNA KAGURAZAKA
ART CLUB
AMAZING KICK

DON'T KNOCK IT.
WHY'S THE DRY A BLUR TO ME?

HEY! WHAT'D YOU JUST WRITE IN YOUR STUDENT LIST!
COME ON, LET'S SEE!
NOTHING!
JUST A NOTE!
NEGI-KUN? WHERE'D YOU GET THAT HICKEY FROM?

2-A STUDENT PROFILE

STUDENT NUMBER 8
ASUNA KAGURAZAKA (LEFT)

BIRTHDATE: APRIL 21, 1988
BLOODTYPE: B
FAVORITE THINGS: TAKAHATA-SENSEI, COOL MEN
DISLIKES: KIDS, STUDYING
CLUB ACTIVITIES: ART CLUB

STUDENT NUMBER 13
KONOKA KONOE (RIGHT)

BIRTHDATE: MARCH 18, 1989
BLOODTYPE: AB
FAVORITE THINGS: FORTUNE-TELLING, THE SUPERNATURAL, COOKING
DISLIKES: ALMOST NONE
CLUB ACTIVITIES: FORTUNE-TELLING CLUB, LIBRARY EXPLORATION CLUB
REMARKS: SCHOOL DEAN'S GRANDDAUGHTER

3RD PERIOD BATHHOUSE RUB♡

MAHORA ACADEMY STUDENT DORMITORY
643 ASUNA KAGURAZAKA
KONOKA KONOE
NEGI
DING DONG
WHO COULD IT BE THIS LATE?
I'M COMING.
ピポポポ
DING DONG
WE'VE GOT SOME QUESTIONS ABOUT TODAY'S LESSON!
GOOD EVENING, NEGI-SENSEI.
カリ
CHAK
NEO MOBIZAI

EVENING, SIR.
YADDA YADDA
ワイワイ
YOU WANT SOME-THING TO DRINK?
WELL, OKAY. C'MON IN, I GUESS.
QUES-TIONS? SURE.
HEY!
I'M STUDYING!
EVENING.
OH...
NODOKA-SAN... HARUNA-SAN... YUE-SAN.
SO THIS IS WHERE NEGI-SENSEI HANGS HIS HAT, HUH?
WELL, WELL! QUITE THE LITTLE PARTY!
WAMM
WELL... IT'S ABOUT PAGE 86.
SO WHAT'S UP?
KONOKA/ A GINGER ALE, MAYBE?
YADDA
...
DING DONG DING DONG
TUMP
TUMP
TUMP
YAP
ワイ
WELL, THAT GOES WITHOUT SAYING.
YAP
ワイ♡
すすっ
FSH
I CAN THINK OF A FEW QUESTIONS MYSELF. BETTER THAN YOURS, I'D BET.
REALLY? COUNT ME IN.
YAP
キャッ
YAP
キャッ♡
IT'S NOT A "PARTY," REP. IT'S A STUDY GROUP.

THOK
GET OUTTA HERE!
YAP
NOW AN ADVERB IS WHAT AGAIN...?
YAP
ANY CANDY AROUND HERE?
SO IN THE ADVERB FORM...
イライライラ...
URRRRR...
...THIS PLACE IS A DORM FOR ALL THE GIRLS.
SORRY. GUESS I SHOULD HAVE REALIZED...
I HAVE TO STUDY AND GET UP AT THE CRACK OF DAWN! GEEZ!
THE 2ND YEAR STUDENTS ALL LIVE ON THE 5TH AND 6TH FLOOR.
NEGI ASUNA KONOKA
吹き抜け
屋上へ
WELL, DUH. THIS IS A BOARDING SCHOOL...
5-6 F SECOND YEAR STUDENTS
3-4 F FIRST YEAR STUDENTS
2 F SEMINAR ROOMS, MEETING ROOMS, COUNSELING COMMITTEE ROOM
1 F STUDENT HEALTH CARE, MAIN HALL, EXHIBITION HALL
3F BATH HALL, LAUNDRY ROOM
2F STUDENT SHOP
1F STUDENT COOP
B1 CAFETERIA

HUH. SO ALL THE 2-A'S ARE ON THIS FLOOR...
WHOA! THERE'S AN OBSERVATORY! I'D LOVE TO SEE THAT!
NO PROBLEM.
HM?
SNIF SNIF...
?
NO OFFENSE, BUT...
...WHEN DID YOU LAST BATHE?
UHM...
URK
ASUNA-SAN? WHAT'S WRONG ...?
UH... WELL...
THINGS HAVE BEEN SO CRAZY SINCE I GOT HERE... THERE'S BEEN NO TIME...
THEN GRAB ONE IN THE BATH HALL.
IT'S PROBABLY EMPTY NOW.
BUT...
SEE...
I'M...
WHAT?
MMBL
MMBL
REALLY?
ASUNA! HE SAYS HE HATES BATHS!
...
...
SNAPP

AIEEE
YOU'RE NOT STINKING UP MY DORM ROOM!
SHLIP
SHLIP
I'LL BE DOWN LATER.
ARRGH
C'MERE, PIP-SQUEAK!
BESIDES, YOU'RE JUST A KID!
FAIR'S FAIR! YOU'VE SEEN ME NAKED!
BATH HALL "RYOFU"
OH... NO... PLEASE.
PLISSH
GULP
AIEEE
NOW GET IN THERE!
...?
IS THIS ANY WAY TO TREAT A TEACHER?

IT'S THE BATH HALL, DUMMY.
WHOA! WHAT IS THIS!?
HERE. SOAP. TOWEL.
NEED ME TO DO IT FOR YOU?
YOU CAN GET 100 PEOPLE IN AT A TIME, IT'S SO HUGE.
NOW GET BATHING.
I SAW ONE LIKE THIS IN A BOOK ONCE!
IT'S AMAZING!
TUNK
AIEE
IT'S SCENTED SOAP! I'LL SMELL LIKE A GIRL!
PLISH
PLISH
GET BACK HERE!
URGH...
FP...
FP...
FP...
HUH...
FP...

ARE YOU REALLY 10 YEARS OLD?
SO HELPLESS YOU CAN'T EVEN WASH YOUR HAIR.
SQUISHH
RUBB
RUBB
BOY OH BOY...
ARGH
WELL... ON MY 10TH YEAR...
MEANING YOU'RE REALLY NINE? CRIPES!
AGGHHH! YOU'RE TEARING MY SCALP OFF!
SKRRCH
SKRRCH
I'M A FREAKIN' BABY-SITTER!
WHY DOES A JUNIOR HIGH GIRL HAVE TO WORK SO HARD?
YOU DELIVER PAPERS? THAT'S NOT AN EASY GIG.
OOOKAY ...HUH?
I HAVE TO GET UP EARLY TO DELIVER PAPERS, SO BE GRATEFUL I'M TAKING THE TIME FOR YOU!
I'M AN ORPHAN.
TO PAY MY WAY.
HERE WE GO.

STAY STILL. ALMOST DONE.

YOUR... PARENTS ARE DEAD?

HEY! SCREW YOUR SYMPATHY I DON'T NEED–
I FEEL SO SORRY FOR YOU!
IT'S NOT THAT... IT...
...IT'S SO SAD, WHAT YOU TOLD ME. IF I WERE IN YOUR SHOES, I'D BE ANGRY ALL THE TIME TOO.
IF YOU START WHINING THAT I HURT YOU–!
WHAT?!
SLIP
WHOA!
WHUD
ARGH
AIEE
THIS IS AWKWARD.
KINDA.
OKAY.
YADDA
YADDA
...
HM?
AW GREAT!
SOMEONE'S COMING IN WAY EARLY!
HUH? WHA–?
YADDA
YADDA
IF THEY SEE US HERE TOGETHER, I'LL NEVER HEAR THE END OF IT!
FIP
FAP
GULP
PLOOSH
HIDE!

ワイワイ...
YADDA
YADDA...
A BATH CLEANSES THE SOUL.
KONOKA... YOU LOOK LIKE YOU WERE EXPECTING TO SEE SOMEONE HERE.
I, UH... GUESS NOT. NO.
OOOO-KAY.
YADDA
YADDA
ワイワイ♡
あうぅ
UNNGH!
ボボボ
ゴボ
GLUG
GLUG...
...THAT NEGI-SENSEI SHOULD BE ROOMING WITH A NUT LIKE ASUNA-SAN...
IT'S SO UNFAIR...
FIGURES/ IT'S REP AND THE OTHERS.

I BET HE'D LET NEGI-SENSEI STAY WITH US IF WE ASKED.
THE DEAN?
SHE'S NOT SO BAD. AND IT'S WHAT GRANDPA WANTED.

THEY'RE DOPES.
WHAT'S UP WITH THEM?

WHAT...
HMP ♥
RIGHT, NODOKA? ♥

LET ME GUESS: SOMEONE LIKE YOU, AYAKA? TO HELP "RAISE HIM" PROPERLY, MAYBE?
YOU GUYS CAN BARELY LOOK AFTER YOURSELVES! HE NEEDS SOMEONE...

THE WOMAN IN CHARGE OF HIM MUST BE A MOTHER FIGURE...
HE MAY BE SMART, BUT NEGI-SENSEI IS STILL A KID.
MMM...

SO HE HAS TO BE RAISED...
HUH ...?

AND, HEY... WHO'S GOT MORE OF A FIGURE THAN ME, RIGHT?
ホホホ HA HA HA
AND WHO'S MORE OF A MOTHER, TOO. GET IT?
YEAH, I GET IT.
IT'S NICE SHE'S SO MATERNAL.
NUDGE NUDGE
ぷよぷよ
コク コク
NOD NOD
OH, YEAH. HER MOTIVES ARE SOOO PURE.
DAMN STRAIGHT!
コク
S-SO AM I CHANGING ROOMS?
I CAN ONLY HOPE.
BU-BUT...
キャイ キャイ
BACK UP! ARE YOU SAYING THERE'S SOMETHING WRONG WITH MY FIGURE? I'M A PERFECT "10."
YEAH, ON A SCALE OF 1 TO 100.
YOU TAKE THAT BACK!
ZHOOP
ガラッ
HEY, Y'ALL. REP. WHAT'S UP?
BOING
ボイーン
KA-KAEDE...

ずーーーん DADOOM
...AYAKA'S BODY, ACTUALLY.
WE WERE, UH... TALKING ABOUT...
?
...!!
SO WE DON'T DISCUSS BOYS ANYMORE? WEIRD.
GOOD EVENING.
!?
BOING
BOING
↑ NO.18 MANA TATSUMIYA
↑ NO. 3 KAZUMI ASAKURA
↑ NO. 21 CHIZURU NABA
NOTHING. IT'S STUPID.
HA HA ホホ
COMPETITION, HUH? WHAT'S THE PRIZE?
WHAAAAAT?
HM?!
あっ
IT'S KINDA CONFUSING, BUT I THINK THE GIRL WITH THE BEST BOOBS GETS NEGI-SENSEI.
I FORGOT HOW... IMPRESSIVE... SOME GIRLS CAN BE.
アハハ...
WHAT A BUNCH OF BOOBS...
ホホホ
HA HA HA
WELCOME TO THE MISS NAKED JAPAN COMPETITION.

YEAHH
ワイ
YEAHH
ワイ
YEAHH
ワイ♡
WHAT? WHAT KIND OF CRAZY CONTEST—!
NO CRAZIER THAN ANYTHING ELSE AROUND HERE!
GETS HIMP HOW?♥
YOU MEAN YOU CAN DO ANYTHING WITH HIM!?
LIKE HAVE HIM DO OUR HOME-WORK!?
YEAH, SURE!!
...
TH-THIS IS GETTING... RIDICU-LOUS.
DOES PERSON-ALITY COUNT AT ALL?
DEPENDS. DO YOU HAVE ONE?
HEY♡
キャ
YAP
WHAT ARE YOUR CHANCES?
HMMM
BETTER THAN YOURS.
キャ♡
YAP
キャ
HMM
NO. 12 FEI KU
NO. 19 LINGSHEN CHAO
NO. 17 SAKURAKO SHIINA
NO. 11 MADOKA KUGIMIYA
NO. 7 MISA KAKIZAKI
NO. 15 TSUNA SAKURAZAKI
AND THE SAME TO YOU.
YEAH. FAR, FAR INTO THE FUTURE, FLAT CHESTS.
HMM
さわ
さわ...
HMM...
HOPE FOR...
...THE FUTURE.
ポー
TUMP
...
NO. 26 EVANGELINE A.K. MCDOWELL
NO. 23 FUMIKA NARUTAKI
NO. 22 FUKA NARUTAKI

UH WAIT...
TUNK
COME ON, NEGI, LET'S GET OUTTA HERE.
HUH.
YADDA
DON'T THEY HAVE ANYTHING BETTER TO DO!
PLISH
WHAT...
OWW
SHLOOP
UNGH
A-ASUNA !?
WHAT ARE YOU DOING ON TOP OF HIS HALF-NAKED BODY!?
ARGH !!
は？！
IT'S NEGI-SENSEI !!
NEGI-SENSEI —!?

EVENING, ALL.
U-UH WELL... THIS IS...
...WITH THE GIRL WITH THE LARGEST BREASTS!!
THIS IS TROUBLE. I'LL END UP STAYING...
WELL, IT SURE WASN'T MY WAY!
IT'S NOT MY WAY!
YOU'RE HAVING YOUR WAY WITH OUR TEACHER ?!?
ALL RIGHT... HERE I GO...
MAK! STER
RAS TER
MA SKIL
GRAB
MY STAFF ...!!
HEY!
WHIRRR
MY SPECIAL WIND MAGIC.
HUH
Aerear amplificet mamas!!
?
RR...

!?
FWOOM
WOW!
TALK ABOUT GROWTH SPURTS!
WH–
WHERE DID THOSE ...?
DID IT WOR...?
PHEW
WH–
NOW WHAT?!
FWOOOM
UH OH.
BLAMMM
OHHH BOY.
AREEEE
ARRRGH
AW, C'MON!
THEY'RE BALLOONS, YOU MORONS!
WOWWW
ASUNA'S GOT US ALL BEAT!

KONOKA KONOE
NEGI
GET HIM OUT!
...IN A WAY THAT WOULD LET ME STAY WITH YOU.
BUT THEY DID, RIGHT?
I JUST ASKED THE MAGIC TO RESOLVE THE PROBLEM...
IF THEY HADN'T SNAPPED BACK TO NORMAL—!
HE TURNED MY BREASTS INTO BALLOONS!
B-BUT—
UNGH...
THIS WAY YOU CAN DESTROY MY LIFE 24/7!
OF COURSE YOU WANT TO STAY HERE!
WOULD YOU LIKE TINY BREASTS? 'CAUSE THAT'S NO PROB—
ASUNA, HE DOESN'T KNOW ANY BETTER. FORGET ABOUT IT AND COME OUT OF THE BATHROOM.
SHUT UP!!
TUMP
TUMP
TUMP
TUMP
I SWEAR, ASUNA-SAN, I'LL BE MUCH MORE CAREFUL NEXT TIME!
CHUD
Toilet
NUTS!

2-A STUDENT PROFILE

STUDENT NUMBER 4
YUE AYASE (LEFT)

BIRTHDATE: NOVEMBER 16, 1988
BLOODTYPE: AB
FAVORITE THINGS: READING
DISLIKES: STUDYING FOR SCHOOL
CLUB ACTIVITIES: CHILDREN'S LITERATURE STUDY GROUP,
PHILOSOPHY STUDY GROUP,
LIBRARY CLUB

STUDENT NUMBER 14
HARUNA SAOTOME (RIGHT)

BIRTHDATE: AUGUST 18, 1988
BLOODTYPE: B
FAVORITE THINGS: TEA CEREMONY;
LOTS OF TROUBLE
DISLIKES: REPTILES, DEADLINES
CLUB ACTIVITIES: MANGA CLUB,
LIBRARY EXPLORATION
GROUP
REMARKS: PSEUDONYM "PAL"

STUDENT NUMBER 27
NODOKA MIYAZAKI (MIDDLE)

BIRTHDATE: MAY 10, 1988
BLOODTYPE: O
FAVORITE THINGS: TO BE SURROUNDED BY BOOKS,
ORGANIZING BOOKS
DISLIKES: GUYS
CLUB ACTIVITIES: GENERAL LIBRARY COMMITTEE MEMBER,
LIBRARY REPRESENTATIVE,
LIBRARY CLUB

4TH PERIOD
THE DREADED AFTERSCHOOL SESSION!

I'M OUTTA HERE!
HOLD UP, ASUNA-CHAN!
MAICHO NEWS
MAI 毎朝新聞
朝新聞
CHO NEWS
チュンチュン..
I DON'T SUPPOSE YOU COULD... NAH, IT'S TOO MU–
OYAMA-KUN JUST CALLED IN SICK.
TAKE HIS ROUTE? NO SWEAT.
...AND A GIRL AT THAT. ARE YOU SURE–?
THAT'S DOUBLE YOUR ROUTE/ YOU'RE A JUNIOR HIGH KID...
チチチ..
CHIRP CHIRP

SURE? I WAS BORN SURE, WITH THE STRENGTH OF TEN KIDS!
I'M ON IT!
MORNING, OFFI-CERS!
HEY THERE, NEWS GIRL.
SHE'S SUCH A GOOD GIRL.
WISH WE HAD A DAUGHTER LIKE HER.
SAME HERE.
CAN'T EVEN SLEEP ANYMORE.
GRRR
MAN... STILL YAWNING...
THANKS TO NEGI, I'M IN "PARTY CENTRAL..."
MAI
MAN, THIS WEIGHS A TON.
FWOM
CARE FOR A LIFT, ASUNA?

ふわっ…
FOOM...
HUH...
FINALLY FIGURED A FOOL-PROOF WAY...
...TO MAKE YOUR LIFE EASIER.
WHOA—!
YOU CAN FLY ?!?
MA!

WOW!! AFTER ALL THE STUPID TRICKS, HERE'S REAL, USEFUL, AMAZING MAGIC!
JUST... NO QUIDDITCH JOKES, OKAY?
YUP. YOU'LL FINISH YOUR ROUTE IN NO TIME.
ハ!TP
HEY, IT WON'T FLY.
PSH
ぷすんっ
SH
ぷすんっ
ひゅるるる
FWEE
FWOM
HUH?
WOW-
ゴオオッ
RRR
HOLD ON! UP, UP AND AWAY!
HM? BUT... IF YOU'RE SEEN...
WE'LL BE A BLUR. NO SWEAT.
HAVE A SEAT.
...
ポコッ
THOK
HOW MUCH DO YOU WEIGH, ASUNA-SAN?
THAT'S WEIRD.
120kg くらい?
EEEEEEE...
STOP HELPING ME!
ドガガッシャ
KRRRSH
GRRR
プン プン
WAIT UP, WILL YOU PL-
RRRRRR
...TO IMPLY YOU'RE FAT!
AW, C'MON, ASUMA-SAN! I DIDN'T MEAN...
ゴビュ
FWEEE

643 ASUNA KAGURAZAKA
KONOKA KONOE
NEGI

I'VE HAD IT UP TO HERE WITH THAT BRAT.

MUCH MORE OF HIS HELP...

ニャー

FSSHH

AND HE'LL HELP ME OUT OF A JOB! OR THE SCHOOL!

FWOM
FWOM...
HUH?
FWEEE
I'LL USE MAGIC...
TO ENSURE HER...
...THE MOST ENJOY-ABLE BATH EVER!
HEY...
STOP IT! THAT... THAT TICKLES!
FP FP
AIEEE
HA HA HA HA
RUBB
RUBB
UHM...
WHAT'S GOT ASUNA SO WIRED?
HAA AHA HAHA HA
RUBB
RUBB
BWAAA HA HA HA
BONG
BONG
BONG
AIEEE
WHUD
WHUD
I'LL KICK YOU TO OSAKA FOR THIS!

AND AN EVEN WORSE TEACHER. MAYBE...
THIS IS HOPELESS. I'M A LOUSY MAGICIAN...
HOW'S THE KID INSTRUCTOR?
HE SEEMS DOWN.
I WONDER WHAT'S WRONG.
...I SHOULD GIVE UP MY JOB...AND MY STAFF. NO MORE MAGIC. THEN...
!
NO...
TAKAHATA-SENSEI WANTED ME TO GIVE YOU THE "AFTER-SCHOOL SESSION LIST FOR CLASS 2-A."
CAN I HELP YOU?
OH... SHIZUNA-SENSEI. HELLO.
THAT'S THE SPIRIT, NEGI-SENSEI.
NO... I CAN'T JUST QUIT.

...AND LOW SCORERS STAY AFTER SCHOOL FOR TUTORING.
YES, TAKAHATA-SENSEI GIVES POP QUIZZES...
"AFTER-SCHOOL SESSION LIST"?

ACCEPT AFTER SCHOOL HELP? WELL, SHE'S NEVER MINDED BEFORE...
ASUNA-SAN COULD SURE USE ENGLISH HELP, BUT SHE'D NEVER—

LET'S SEE WHO THE LUCKY DEVILS ARE.
IT'S YOUR JOB, IF YOU THINK YOU CAN HANDLE IT.

Afterschool Session List
No. 4 Yue Ayase
Quiz 7 8 Points
Quiz 8 14 Points
No. 8 Asuna Kagurazaka
Quiz 7 6 Points
Quiz 8 8 Points
No. 12 Fei Ku
Quiz 7 12 Points
Quiz 8 14 Points
No. 16 Makie Sasaki
Quiz 7 8 Points
Quiz 8 10 Points
OF COURSE.

I'VE FINALLY FOUND A WAY TO HELP ASUNA-SAN!
YES! PERFECT!
WAAIT A MINUTE. MAYBE...

YEAH, I GUESS SO.
THEN AGAIN, TAKAMICHI TAUGHT THOSE. YOU, IT'D BE A DIFFERENT STORY.

* BAKA = IDIOT IN JAPANESE.

EVERY-ONE READY?
OKAY-♡
BEGIN.
SKRCH
カリカリ
SKRCH
YOU STAY UNTIL YOU SCORE AT LEAST 6 POINTS.
FIRST OFF...A TEN POINT QUIZ.
BRING IT-♡
OH FOR GOD'S SAKE...
キャー
HURRAH
AAAAND... GREAT! NINE POINTS! GOOD FOR YUE... UH...YOU, YUE.
THAT WAS FAST!
HERE Y'GO...
THIS IS MY SMILE.
YOU COULD SMILE ABOUT IT, Y'KNOW...
ME TOO. ♥
I'M DONE TOO.
BOW
ペコッ
SORRY. WHAT WAS I THINKING?
SH'RIGHT.
AND JUST THINK! IF YOU ACTUALLY STUDIED-!

ちょーーん
UHH

...
ぐいっ
FIP...

UH...
ASUNA-SAN? HOW'S IT GOING?

"I AM," "YOU ARE," "HE IS..."
THEN WE'LL TRY ANOTHER QUIZ. FIRST, "TO BE."
UH HUH...
OKAY-♥
OKAY, LADIES, LET'S WORK ON VERB DECLENSIONS.

CONGRATS! YOU'RE OUTTA HERE!
KAEDE NAGASE, FEI KU... BOTH EIGHT POINTS!

WE'RE DONE.
URR, IT SHOULD BE TAKAHATA-SENSEI TELLING ME THIS...
NO, SEE, IT'S "THEY ARE," NOT "THEY AM..."

I'LL DO EVEN BETTER NEXT TIME.
RIFFLE くしゃくしゃ
YOU SQUEAKED BY WITH SIX, MAKIE.
"PROFESSOR." I'M DONE.
HA HA HA
I CHINESE. SPEAKING JAPANESE HARD ENOUGH!
DADOOM どーん
DOOM スッ
LE-LET'S SEE, THAT LEAVES US WITH ASUNA-SAN.
AGAIN, "TO BE." "I AM," "YOU ARE"...
KILL ME NOW.
...YOU CAN NAIL ENGLISH IN NO TIME FLAT!
OKAY! NO SWEAT! IF I CAN MASTER JAPANESE IN THREE WEEKS...
KAHH アホー
KAHH アホー
HEY, HOW'S IT GOING, NEGI-KUN?
AW, DON'T GIVE UP ASUNA-SAN.
I ARE STUPID, YOU AM USELESS...
ず〜ん
DADOOM

NOT... ON PURPOSE, BUT...
TAKAHATA-SENSEI...
DOOM
HA HA...
BEING A PAIN IN THE ASS FOR NEGI, ARE YOU?
ASUNA-KUN. SHOULD'VE KNOWN.
TA-
HA HA HA
WHAT-EVER! KEEP AT IT!
BUT...
...
SHUMP...
URR URR...
ASUNA-SAN...
...IT'S GONNA BE FINE...
WAIT, ASUNA-SAN!
FWOOSH
WOW, SHE'S FAST.
HUH !?
BUT I'M FASTER!
FWOOM...
TMP
IT'S NEVER GONNA BE FINE!

ASUNA-SAN! GET BACK HERE!
WHYP! THERE'S NO POINT!
FWICH
FWOOSH
HE DOES NOT!
AW, ASUNA-SAN—!
TAKAHATA-SENSEI THINKS I'M A JOKE!
AND HE'S RIGHT!
I AM!
AGUNA!
ASUNA-SAN!
FICH...
HUF
HUF
HUF
HUF
FSSSH
...AND I SWEAR...
YOU...
...YOU COME NEAR ME, NEGI...
...SO FAR UP YOUR... YOUR...
I'LL SHOVE THAT STAFF...
HUF... はあ...
HUF はあ
SHLUMP...
HUF... へたり...
HUF へたり...

MEET ASUNA KAGURAZAKA, DEAD GIRL WALKING.
AW, C'MON...
OBVIOUSLY YOUR HELPING ME MEANS KILLING ME WITH KINDNESS.
OH, I GIVE UP.
HUF HUF...
AFTER ALL, A MASTER MAGUS' JOB IS TO HELP OTHERS, SO...
ACTUALLY, WE CAN HELP EACH OTHER.
NO, TO... HIM.
BUT WHO'RE YOU TRYING TO PROVE IT TO? YOURSELF?
KIND OF.
SO YOU'RE TRYING TO PROVE YOU'RE GOOD ENOUGH?
OH, SWELL...
...WHO SOME NOW SAY IS DEAD. BUT I THINK...
TUGG
...NOT.
THE MAN WHO GAVE ME THIS STAFF. THE MAN WHO...

HE'S CALLED THE "THOUSAND MASTER," BECAUSE HE MASTERED A THOUSAND MAGIC SPELLS.
HE TRAVELS THE WORLD SAVING COUNTLESS INNOCENTS. AND HE APPEARED TO ME ONE DAY, OUT OF THE BLUE...
I'LL NEVER FORGET WHAT HE SAID.
YOU'VE GROWN, NEGI. HERE... TAKE THIS, SO YOU'LL GROW MORE...
...BE WATCHING YOU.
AND KNOW THAT I WILL ALWAYS...

I'D NEVER HAVE GRADUATED MAGIC SCHOOL WITHOUT IT. AND IF I KEEP STUDYING...
...MY KNOWLEDGE WILL SOMEDAY MATCH ITS POWER. ON THAT DAY, I KNOW HE'LL RETURN... AND SAY, "WELL DONE."
...
HMM
くしゃ SKRITCH SKRITCH くしゃ
...
...WELL ...GOOD.
OH! UH...
I'LL STUDY, OKAY !?
FINE, YOU WIN!

ガリガリガリ
SKRCH SKRCH...
DEAL?
I FIGURE I DON'T NEED YOU BLAMING MY LOUSY GRADES...
...FOR PREVENTING YOU FROM BECOMING THIS MAGI THING.

DON'T HUG ME, YOU IDIOT.
AND YOU WON'T REGRET—!
DEAL ...!
SURE ...!

THERE! YOU WANT TEN ANSWERS RIGHT?

TEN ON ONE TEST, ASUNA, NOT FOUR ADDED TOGETHER.
WELL WHAT?
...AHEM...
DON'T TELL ME...!
3
4
5
3

WELL, UH...
GRADE IT YOUR-SELF!
YEAHH
YOU GOT TEN ANSWERS RIGHT!
HA HA

2-A STUDENT PROFILE

STUDENT NUMBER 2
YUNA AKASHI (BOTTOM)

BIRTHDATE: JUNE 1, 1988
BLOODTYPE: A
FAVORITE THINGS: FATHER
DISLIKES: BAD CLOTHES,
SHIRTS HANGING OUT,
SLOPPY LIFESTYLE
CLUB ACTIVITIES: BASKETBALL

STUDENT NUMBER 5
AKO IZUMI (RIGHT)

BIRTHDATE: NOVEMBER 21, 1988
BLOODTYPE: A
FAVORITE THINGS: CUTE BANDAIDS,
DOING LAUNDRY
DISLIKES: BLOOD, FIGHTS
CLUB ACTIVITIES: NURSE'S OFFICE,
BOYS' SOCCER
TEAM MANAGER

STUDENT NUMBER 16
MAKIE SASAKI (TOP LEFT)

BIRTHDATE: MARCH 7, 1989
BLOODTYPE: O
FAVORITE THINGS: DEVOTED TO RHYTHMIC GYMNASTICS,
NEGI, CUTE THINGS
DISLIKES: SLIMY THINGS LIKE NATTO
CLUB ACTIVITIES: RHYTHMIC GYMNASTICS

5TH PERIOD SUPER DODGE BALL COMPETITION!!
~GO GIRLS! (PART ONE)

YEAHH
YEAHH
YEAHH
IN THE AIR!
GET THE BALL!
TUM
TUM
HE'S OKAY. GOT THE WHOLE "CUTE" THING GOING FOR HIM...
HE SURE TRIES HARD, DOESN'T HE.
WHAT DO YOU GUYS THINK OF HIM?
TUM
HM
SO NEGI-KUN'S HERE NEARLY A WEEK...

NEGI'S TEN/ WHAT'LL HE ADVISE US ON? HIDE AND SEEK?
YEAH, BUT AN ADULT TEACHER CAN ADVISE YOU ON STUFF.
AW, C'MON, THE HIGH SCHOOL HERE TAKES US AUTOMATICALLY, SO IT'S NO SWEAT.
BUT WITH ENTRANCE EXAMS NEXT YEAR, DON'T WE NEED SOMEONE WHO DOES MORE THAN TRY HARD?

DON'T YOU AGREE?
NOT COMPARED TO ME, YOU WOULDN'T.
AIEE!

DON'T YOU GUYS THINK I'D BE GOOD AT THAT?
!

I COULD BE HIS SURROGATE BIG SISTER!
バシ
WAP
ACTUALLY, NEGI-KUN MIGHT HAVE TO COME TO US FOR ADVICE
WHOA
ぷぷぷぷ
TEE HEE

YOU'RE ...!!
YO-

MMBL ざわ
MMBL ざわ
JUNIOR HIGH FACULTY OFFICE

NEGI-SENSEI.
YES, MA'AM?
I FIGURED NOW IS A GOOD TIME TO ASK YOU...
DO YOU THINK YOU'RE READY TO FLY SOLO?
THAT'S HOW I USUALLY FLY...
OH, AS A TEACHER! NO, NOT YET. I THINK THEY DON'T SEE ME AS AN AUTHORITY FIGURE BECAUSE, Y'KNOW, OF MY AGE...
HA HA... WELL, THAT'S TOO BAD.
WE WERE ATTACKED...
えーん AIEEE
LOOK AT THESE BRUISES!! HELP US!!
NEGI-SENSEI-!! TAKE CHARGE!
USE YOUR AUTHORITY!
ガラ
UH-OH.
WH-WHAT ...!?
WHO WOULD DO THAT ...!?

WOW!
AH
THONK
IT'S ME, EIKO THE HIGH SCHOOL ACE!!
WAK
KRICH...
YOU'RE JUST LITTLE BABIES COMPARED TO US HIGH SCHOOL GIRLS!
HA HA SO YOU SEE?
YOU HEARD HER! LEGGO!
GET YOUR HANDS OFF ME!
SHLIPP
NOW CRAWL ASIDE, BABIES.
OHHH, NEGI-SENSEI'S DEAD.

GIRLS! CHECK THIS OUT!
...
YOU'RE KIDDING.
!!
ALL OF YOU, KEEP BACK...
FICH
FICH...
IS THAT HIM?
DON'T MAKE ME ANGRY! YOU... YOU WOULDN'T LIKE ME WHEN I'M ANGRY!
HOW DARE YOU PICK ON MY GIRLS! I'M THEIR INSTRUCTOR!
BUT I THOUGHT IT WAS A JOKE! AND I HADN'T HEARD HOW ADORABLE HE WAS!
I'D HEARD ABOUT A 10-YEAR-OLD INSTRUCTOR...
!?
WHOOSH
WOW-♥ HE'S SO CUTE!
YO! GIRLS! TAKE A COLD SHOWER!
WONK
OOF
DAMN MY CHARISMA!
YAP YAP
YEAHH YEAHH
THERE'S PLENTY OF HIM FOR ALL!
NO, I'M FIRST.
I'M GOING TO HOLD HIM FIRST.
MAW
CRIPES! I'M A FREAKIN' GIRL MAGNET!

ASUNA-SAN AND THE REP!?
FICH
WHAT WAS THAT!?
WH...
HM?
TOUGH TALK FOR A TODDLER!
YOU GIRLS HAVE YOUR OWN HANGOUT. SO TAKE OFF. DON'T MAKE US GET VIOLENT.
THIS FIELD'S RESERVED FOR 2-A USE.
THERE'S NO "WE" NEEDED. I'LL KICK YOUR ASSES BACK SINGLE-HANDED... FOOTED... WHATEVER!
ONE SIDE, AYAKA.
BIG TALK FOR AN ANCIENT!
OOF
BUT YOUR JUNIOR HIGH REP MEANS SQUAT TO US HIGH SCHOOL GIRLS.
ASUNA KAGURAZAKA AND AYAKA YUKIHIRO. TOUGH TALKERS.
I'M SHAKING IN MY STYLISH SHOES.

WE RUN THINGS AROUND HERE. WE GO WHERE WE WANT, DO WHAT WE WANT...
...TO WHOMEVER WE WANT. GOT THAT, ASUNA?
DOOOM
HMPH
AND RIGHT NOW, WE WANT TO DO THINGS WITH CUTIE HERE.
TEE HEE
GET YOUR HANDS OFF ME.
GRRR
YOU HEARD HIM, YOU OLD HAG!
RIII

TAKA-HATA-SENSEI...!?
FWOOSH
MI-
FOOSH
AND YOU LADIES! MY FORMER STUDENTS...
YE-YES SIR...
SAVE YOUR ENERGY FOR YOUR STUDIES OKAY? YOU NEED IT.
NO, SIR.
U-UH...
YOUR BEHAVIOR SHAMES ME. WAS THAT YOUR GOAL, TO SHAME ME?
HE MADE RESOLVING THIS LOOK EASY!
WO-WOW, TAKAMICHI'S AMAZING.
THE PROVOCATION, YES. BUT IF YOU LET IT GET TO YOU, EVERYONE LOSES.
THIS WAS ALL THEIR FAULT!
LET'S GO.

HE'LL BE MY ROLE MODEL.
HMM. HE'S A REAL TEACHER.
I WISH I COULD'VE HANDLED IT LIKE YOU.
HA HA HA
TAKES PRACTICE, THAT'S ALL.
JUNIOR HIGH 2ND YEAR CLASS A
キャイ キャイ
YAP
YAP
DON'T YOU THINK TAKAHATA-SENSEI'S AWESOME?
YEAH...
NOTHING THROWS HIM.
WHAT HAPPENED?
OH, THE SENIORS WERE TRYING TO GRAB TERRITORY.
OH NO-, NOT AGAIN.
THEY'VE BEEN PULLING THAT ON EVERY-ONE.

NEGI WASN'T MUCH USE.
WHAT'D YOU EXPECT?
HEY! WHAT HAPPENED TO THINKING HE'S ADORABLE?!
HMPH!
GET A GRIP, AYAKA.
URRR
HE'S A KID, REMEMBER?
VOLLEYBALL ON THE ROOF COURT TODAY, RIGHT?
SO LET'S GET GOING.
YADDA ワイ
YADDA ワイ
OKAY-
SEEING MR. TAKAHATA-SENSEI IN ACTION REMINDS YOU WHAT A REAL TEACHER IS LIKE,
CUTENESS ONLY GOES SO FAR.
THIS SCHOOL'S GETTING WAY OVER-CROWDED. THAT'S THE BIG PROBLEM.
REC SPACE, COURT SPACE, STUDY SPACE...
EVERYTHING'S IN SHORT SUPPLY.
TOTALLY.
HUH?
HEY...

HELLOOO, LADIES.
FANCY MEETING YOU HERE.

YES, FANCY THAT..
HIGH SCHOOL CLASS 2-D!

WHAT ARE YOU DOING ON THEIR SIDE, NEGI-SENSEI!!
I'M SUPPOSED TO BE SUBBING FOR YOUR GYM TEACHER! AND THESE BEHEMOTHS FOUND ME HERE!

WE HAVE A FREE PERIOD, SO WE'RE PLAYING VOLLEYBALL.
IT'S OUR GYM CLASS NOW!
SEEMS WE'RE DOUBLE BOOKED THEN.

LOOK! OVER THERE! IT'S...
...NEGI?

FIRST COME, FIRST SERVED, LADIES.
WE CAME FIRST, SO IT'S OUR SERVE.
YOU DID THIS ON PURPOSE!
YOUR BUILDING HAS ITS OWN ROOF COURT!
WHY COME HERE AND USE OURS ?!

BUT THE VIEW HERE IS SO MUCH NICER! WE CAN SEE YOUR BABY FACES MORE CLEARLY! ♥
THAT'S IT! SHE'S HIS-TORY!
YOU TELL 'EM!
YEAH! THEY'RE THE ONES ACTING LIKE BABIES!

I HAVE TO STOP THIS FIGHT SOME-HOW...
BUT TAKAMICHI ISN'T AROUND SO WHAT DO I DO...!?

SOME-ONE SHOULD CHANGE YOUR DIAPERS, ASUNA!
キャー
RIEEE
ワ
YEAHHH
キッ
AHHH
DON'T TAKE THAT, ASUNA!
SMACK HER INTO NEXT WEEK!
SHOW HER WHAT YOU'VE GOT!
PUT NEGI-SENSEI DOWN! NOW!

AH...
AH...
ふわっ
EWOM...
WHAT?

HM
ムズ ムズ...
URR URR...

AH CHOO!!!
WHOA...
AIEEE...
KRAK
...VIOLENCE IS NO WAY TO RESOLVE AN ARGUMENT!
EXCUSE ME BUT...
...HUH!
YEAH. FREAKY.
FREAKY WEATHER WE'VE HAD LATELY, HUH?
OH MY...
BOY...

WHOSE FACE DO WE GET TO TEAR OFF?
INSTEAD OF ENDLESS ARGUING, EVERYTHING GETS RESOLVED IN ONE BIG FACE OFF!
I SUGGEST THIS BE SETTLED... SPORTINGLY.
SINCE YOU ALL LIKE SPORTS SO MUCH...
THAT SEEMS FAIR. RIGHT, NEGI-SENSEI?
WINNER HAS FIRST DIBS ON ALL THE DISPUTED TERRITORIES.
JUUUUST KIDDING. SURE. WE'LL PLAY.
FINE WITH US SENIORS, PROFESSOR. WE'LL EVEN SPOT THEM 11 EXTRA PLAYERS.
I SUGGEST DODGE BALL!
CONSIDERING YOUR PHYSICAL DIFFERENCES...
OKAY GIRLS, UH...I NEVER SAID IT HAD TO BE VOLLEYBALL.
AND THAT'S OUR FAULT HOW, EXACTLY?
FAIR?! YOU'RE, LIKE, TWICE AS BIG AS US!
THEY'LL BE SORRY!
YOU BET!
YOU'RE ON! RIGHT, GIRLS!
THINK FASTER!
LEMME THINK...

I... I DO ...?
...IF WE WIN, NEGI-SENSEI TRANSFERS TO OUR SCHOOL TO TEACH.
BUT...
TUGG
ARGH
OHHH, AYAKA-SAN, I HOPE YOU KNOW WHAT YOU'RE DOING!
DEAL!
FOOM
FAFOOM
RICKUM RACKUM RUCKUM RUCKUM!
THROW THAT BALL AND REALLY F... ...FIGHT!
WE'RE DOOMED.
NO KID-DING.
FOOM

FICH

SAINT URSULA GIRLS' HIGH SCHOOL 2-D OF MAHORA ACADEMY

VS.

MAHORA GIRLS' JUNIOR HIGH

BABOOM

SPECIAL GUEST: NEGI-SENSEI

I CAUGHT THE REBOUND, NEGI-SENSEI!
YOU'RE STILL IN! DON'T SCREW UP!
COME ON!
ARRGH
OOOOF!
THUNK
FAH
FWOOSH
GOOD GOING, ASUNA! ♥
YOU'RE OUT !!
THUNK
OUCH
YOU BET!
GREAT! SHOW THEM BEFORE I GET KILLED, OKAY?!
NEGI
LET'S SHOW THEM HOW IT'S DONE!

6TH PERIOD SUPER DODGE BALL COMPETITION!! ~GO GIRLS! (PART TWO)

OKAY, TEAM! FAILURE IS NOT AN OPTION!
WE'LL TEACH THEM TO UNDER-ESTIMATE US JUST 'CAUSE WE'RE YOUNGER!
YOU? TEACH US?
OHHH, I DON'T THINK SO.
NOW NEGI TEACHING US IS MORE LIKELY. AFTER WE WIN, OF COURSE.
SHE CREEPS ME OUT.
AND SHE'S WAY TOO BIG, REALLY.
SHE'S MOVING AWFULLY FAST!
NOT FAST AS ME!
OKAY, LITTLE POTA-TOES...
TIME TO GET MASHED!
FWOOSH
VWOM
BOING
CLEAR A SPACE!
COMING THROUGH!
THIS IS NO TIME TO PANIC!

AW, GO AHEAD! PANIC!
OUCH
WONK
ボン
OOH
ボーン
TUNK
ボコッ
THUP
TUP
テンッ
テンッ
TUP
URGH

2-A WITH 3 OUTS !!
OOH
SORRY
OWW
HOW'D SHE DO THAT?!

ひょいっ
WOOP
KIND OF LIKE THIS!

GIRLS! IT'S "DODGEBALL!" YOU MIGHT TRY DODGING!
BU-BUT...
...THERE'S TOO MANY OF US TO MOVE!
...NO!
OH...

ボボボーン
WOWOWON
NO
OH
OOH
AIEE

I DIDN'T HEAR YOU OBJECTING WHEN THEY SUGGESTED IT, REP!
HAVING TWICE AS MANY PLAYERS GIVES US A DISADVANTAGE, YOU DOPE!
YOU FOOL!!

どーん
DOOOM
...JUST GIVES THEM MORE, AND EASIER, TARGETS!
CRAP! SHE'S RIGHT! HAVING A LOT OF TEAM-MATES...

GOOD FOR YOU. TOO LATE, BUT GOOD FOR YOU.
HA HA HA...SO YOU'VE CAUGHT ON.

EASY FOR YOU TO SAY!
HUH?!
DO-DON'T CROWD UP! SCATTER AROUND.
CAN I GO HOME NOW?
バラ
SKAT
バラ
SKAT

ボ
ALEEEE
WONK
...OUT OF THEIR MISERY!

TIME TO PUT THE SLOWEST ONES...
FWOOSH
バン
AW MAN, THIS IS TOO EASY.

ASUNA! FOR GOD'S SAKE, DO SOME-THING!
NO-
SHAGGY-HAIR! YOU'RE NEXT.
YOUR POINT BEING. ...?
YOU HIT HER FROM BEHIND!
FU-FUMIKA-!
AIEEE
FWOOOM
BYE BYE!
GRAB
HM?
FWAP
ASUNA THE POWER HOUSE!
JUST DON'T TURN YOUR BACK ON "XENA" OVER THERE!
NO TIME FOR THANKS!
TH-THANKS, ASUNA-SAN!

OKAY, SENIORS!
I'LL SHOW YOU JUST WHAT WE YOUNGER GIRLS CAN DO!
TMP
YAH !!
THUNK
FWOOOM!
WHIRRR
ABOUT WHAT I EXPECTED.
DOOOM
STOP CALLING ME THAT !!
SHE CAUGHT POWERHOUSE ASUNA'S THROW LIKE IT WAS A FRISBEE!
WHA-T !?
NEGI
BUT YOUR FORM SUCKED.
SIZZZ
"A" FOR EFFORT...
"POWER-HOUSE?" POWER-MOUSE, MORE LIKE.
'CAUSE WE HAPPEN TO BE...
HA HA HA...
FACT IS, KIDDIES... YOU HAVE NO CHANCE AGAINST US.

...THE BLACK LILIES!
...THE KANTO REGIONAL CHAMPION MAHORA DODGE BALL TEAM...
FWO
THERE'S A CHAMPIONSHIP DODGEBALL TEAM?!?
WHAT...?
OKAY, EIKO!
BIBI, SHII!! TRIANGLE ATTACK.
ON SECOND THOUGHT, WE'LL POUND IT INTO YOU!
HEY! SHOW SOME RESPECT!
WHO KNEW? I THOUGHT JUST REAL LITTLE KID'S PLAYED DODGEBALL!
YEAH, AND I THINK WE'RE LOOKIN' AT 'EM!
WERE THE PREVIOUS CHAMPS FIRST-GRADERS?
MMBL
MMBL
MAYBE THEY WERE THE ONLY ONES AT THE TOURNAMENT.
BACK OFF, NEGI-SENSEI. I'LL TAKE THIS ONE!!
DID YOU HEAR THAT? TRIANGLE ATTACK
TEE HEE HEE
HEE
HA HA HA
P

AIEE
I'M IMPRESSED...
NOT!
I, AYAKA YUKIHIRO, CLASS REPRESENTATIVE OF 2-A, SHALL PROTECT NEGI-SENSEI!!
HA HA
ALL RIGHT, CRONES!
YAH
VIP
FWAK
OOH
NICE "PROTECTING," REP!
ARGH
FWAK
TUNK
ONE MORE OUT.
HA HA HA THIS IS A JOKE.
UHHH!
TATUMP
NOW TWO MORE.
OOOF!
11 TO 10.
NEGI TEAM
HIGH SCHOOL GIRLS
11
10
WE SHOULD BE DOING THIS ON ONE LEG!
I'M THINKING TRIANGULAR.
WHAT KIND OF FORMATION... COULD A TRIANGLE ATTACK BE...?
THEIR MOVES WERE... JUST TOO FAST.
FWOM...
A
B
C

THEY'VE CAUGHT UP ALREADY.
WE ARE...
...SO SCREWED...
HAH...
MOST OF THE ONES LEFT ARE EITHER SHRIMPS OR SPAZZES...
ASUNA! YOU'RE THE ONLY WORTHWHILE ONE LEFT!
DEATH-BLOW-
ZING
SUN ATTACK!
WOOSH...
OK!
LADIES! MANEUVER X-2!!
TUMP
SUN'S IN MY EYES-!
DAMMIT!
WAKK

OUCH
THWAK
AIEE
PWAK
ANOTHER ONE BITES THE DUST!
FOOP
A-ASUNA-
ASUNA-SAN!?
ネギ
WHY'D SHE DO THAT!
SHE HIT HER TWICE?!
OWWW... I'VE HAD BETTER DAYS...
A-ARE YOU ALL RIGHT, ASUNA!?
YOU PISS OFF THE BLACK LILIES, YOU PAY!
BECAUSE "POWER-HOUSE" PISSED ME OFF!
MAHORA

ゴオ
WHAT IS...
WHAT...
...THIS WIND !?
オオオッ
RRRRR
BUT NOW... WE'LL SETTLE THEM MY WAY!
I JUST WANTED TO SETTLE THINGS PEACEABLY.
RAS TER MA SKIL
ポッ
VOOP
YOU WERE ALL, "OOOH, FAIR SPORTS COMPETITION!"
THIS WAS YOUR BRIGHT IDEA, REMEMBER?
しゅうう...
SSSHH
KNOCK IT OFF!
HEY, BRAT...
ポカッ
THOK
AER ...!!
OR ARE YOU ONLY HONORABLE WHEN IT'S CONVENIENT?
HOW'S IT FAIR IF WE WIN BY CHEATING, HUH?
...AM ASHAMED...
I...

NO! NOBODY GIVES UP WHILE THERE'S A GAME TO WIN!
WE'VE GOT ZERO CHANCE!
えーん
AEEE
ASUNA'S OUT! WE MIGHT AS WELL QUIT!
FORGET SHAME! JUST GET THE JOB DONE!
A-ASUNA-SAN...
YOU CAN DO THIS!
BE COURA-GEOUS IN YOUR HEARTS... AND YOU CAN PERFORM FEATS OF... OF TRUE MAGIC!
ASUNA'S RIGHT! DON'T RUN OR THEY'LL NAIL YOU FROM BEHIND!
FACE THEM! USE YOUR SKILLS!
GO GO 2-A!!
YOU BET !!!
TO HELL WITH BOTH THOSE OPTIONS!
WE LOSE THE GAME, WE LOSE HIM!
FOR NEGI-SENSEI!
WE HAVE TO DO IT!
HA HA...

...
IF WE LET NEGI-SENSEI DOWN... I DON'T KNOW WHAT I'LL DO...
DAMNED STRAIGHT!
YOU BET!
WE'RE GOING TO WIN THIS, RIGHT!?
NICE PEP TALK, YA LITTLE BRAT.
YEAH!
HERE WE GO!!
KRICH
5 SECOND RULE
TWEED
OH, NEGI. BETTER START WORKING UP A LESSON PLAN FOR THE HIGH SCHOO–
...HUH?
... ...
THAT'S NOT A COMPLIMENT, BY THE WAY.
I'LL SAY THIS FOR YOU! YOU DON'T KNOW WHEN TO GIVE UP!

WHERE WOULD YOU RUNTS GET A RULE-BOOK?!
FORK YOU! YOU JUST MADE THAT UP!

LOST YOUR TURN. FORK OVER THE BALL.
ACCORDING TO THE OFFICIAL RULES, YOU CAN'T HOLD THE BALL OVER 5 SECONDS.

GOOD GOING, BOOK-STORE!
FROM THE LIBRARY WHERE I PRACTICALLY LIVE. SEE?
TWEEP
CRAP!

HAH. I'LL TEACH YOU A LESSON...!
YAHH

TIME TO BEND IT...

YES !!
OUT!
THUNK
OOPS!

UH HUH.
GO, AKIRA-SAN!
NO PROB-LEM.
キラーン
ZING
PASSING THE BALL IS ALSO AGAINST THE RULES, BY THE WAY.

THUNK
ARGH
WHOA!
A CANNON-BALL RETURN FROM THE SOCCER PLAYER!
THOK
...LIKE BECK-HAM!
FOOM...
NICE MOVE, *AIR* YUNA!
I GOT–
–IT ...?!
FP
SWISH
!?
FWAK
ARGH
...ON THE BASKET-BALL TEAM!
THUNK
FWICH
AND HERE'S HOW IT'S DONE...
CHINA DOUBLE ATTACK
YEAHH
YEAHH
AIEEE
AND YOU CRABBED AT US ABOUT STICKING TO THE RULES?!?
NICE, MAKIE! PICK THAT UP IN RHYTHMIC GYMNASTICS, DID YOU?
TOK
TOK
TOK
AIEE
OH!
AIEE
YAH
YAH
YAH

DINGGG
GAME OVER!!
10
03
TIME'S UP!!
WE WON!!
YES!!
...SHE GAVE THEM HOPE.
THAT BITCH ASUNA...
HOW COULD WE LOSE...
SHLUMP
N-NO...
SHE'S GONNA HIT ASUNA-SAN FROM BEHIND!!
!?
FWOOSH
...BY GIVING HER...
I'LL RETURN THE FAVOR...
HUH?
FWOOM!
ASUNA-SAN! DOWN!
A CONCUS-SION!
THOK

FWAK
WHAT...
NEGI ...! ARE YOU ...?
WHIRRRL... ぎゅるるる...
THAT... WASN'T... VERY...
むっ
GRRR
...NICE!
FOOM
!?
WAK

WHAT...
WH-
ZWISSSSH
ZING
SRRRRRIP
!?
OH, CRAP.
HUH...
THAT WAS AMAZING, NEGI-SENSEI!! WHAT WAS THAT!?
YEAHH
UH...
HRURRRRH
MAJ...ESTIC? THE MAJESTIC THROW? IT TOTALLY ROCKED!
UH... MAG— ...UH, MAG—
IT WAS.
YOU SHOULD'VE USED IT SOONER!
WHAT HAPPENED HERE?!?
おお〜
WOW!!
!?
THIS ISN'T FINISHED, BRATS!
あはは
HA HA
HAHH
ガタガタガタ
BRR BRR
I'LL HAVE TO BUY THEM NEW CLOTHES.

CONTINUED IN VOLUME 2

— STAFF —

Ken Akamatsu

Takashi Takemoto

Kenichi Nakamura

Masaki Ohyama

Keiichi Yamashita

Chigusa Amagasaki

Takaaki Miyahara

Kei Nishikawa

Thanks To

Ran Ayanaga

Toshiko Akamatsu

Welcome. . .

. . . to the launch of the Del Rey Manga line! It all starts here, with four new series from Japan: *Negima!* by Ken Akamatsu! *Gundam SEED* by Masatsuga Iwase! And *Tsubasa: Reservoir Chronicle* and *xxxHOLiC*, both by CLAMP! Together, these four series represent some of the best and most popular manga series published in Japan.

We're dedicated to providing our readers with the most enjoyable, authentic manga experience possible. Our books are printed from right to left, in the Japanese printing format. We strive to keep the translations as true to the original as possible, while giving the English versions the same sense of adventure and fun. We keep Japanese honorifics intact, translate all sound effects, and give you extras at the back of the books to help you understand the context of the stories and keep track of all the characters. It's the next best thing to being able to read Japanese yourself!

For information on upcoming releases, visit www.delreymanga.com, and while you're there be sure to sign up for our newsletter. If you do, you'll be the first to hear all the scoop on Del Rey Manga, and you'll have the opportunity to talk back directly to the editor (that would be me) and say what works for you in our books, and what doesn't. Manga wouldn't be the red-hot phenomenon it is without your support, and we want your feedback.

See you in volume 2!

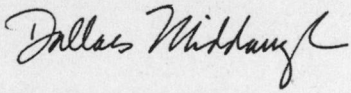

Dallas Middaugh
Director of Manga, Del Rey Books

About the Creator

Negima! is only Ken Akamatsu's third manga, although he started working in the field in 1994 with *AI Ga Tomaranai*. Like all of Akamatsu's work to date, it was published in Kodansha's *Shonen Magazine*. *AI Ga Tomaranai* ran for five years before concluding in 1999. In 1998, however, Akamatsu began the work that would make him one of the most popular manga artists in Japan: *Love Hina*. *Love Hina* ran for four years, and before its conclusion in 2002, it would cause Akamatsu to be granted the prestigious Manga of the Year award from Kodansha, as well as going on to become one of the best-selling manga in the United States.

"PROFESSOR" NEGI, MAGUS
PROVISIONAL 3-A HEIGHT CHART

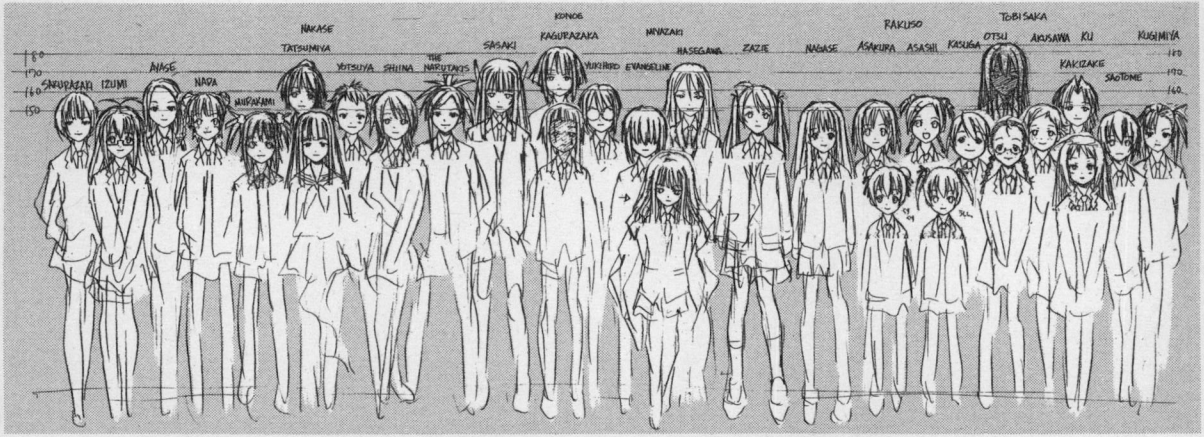

"MAGISTER NEGIMA!" CONCEPT ART COLLECTION

OFFICIAL PROVISIONAL VERSION COMMENTS BY KEN AKAMATSU

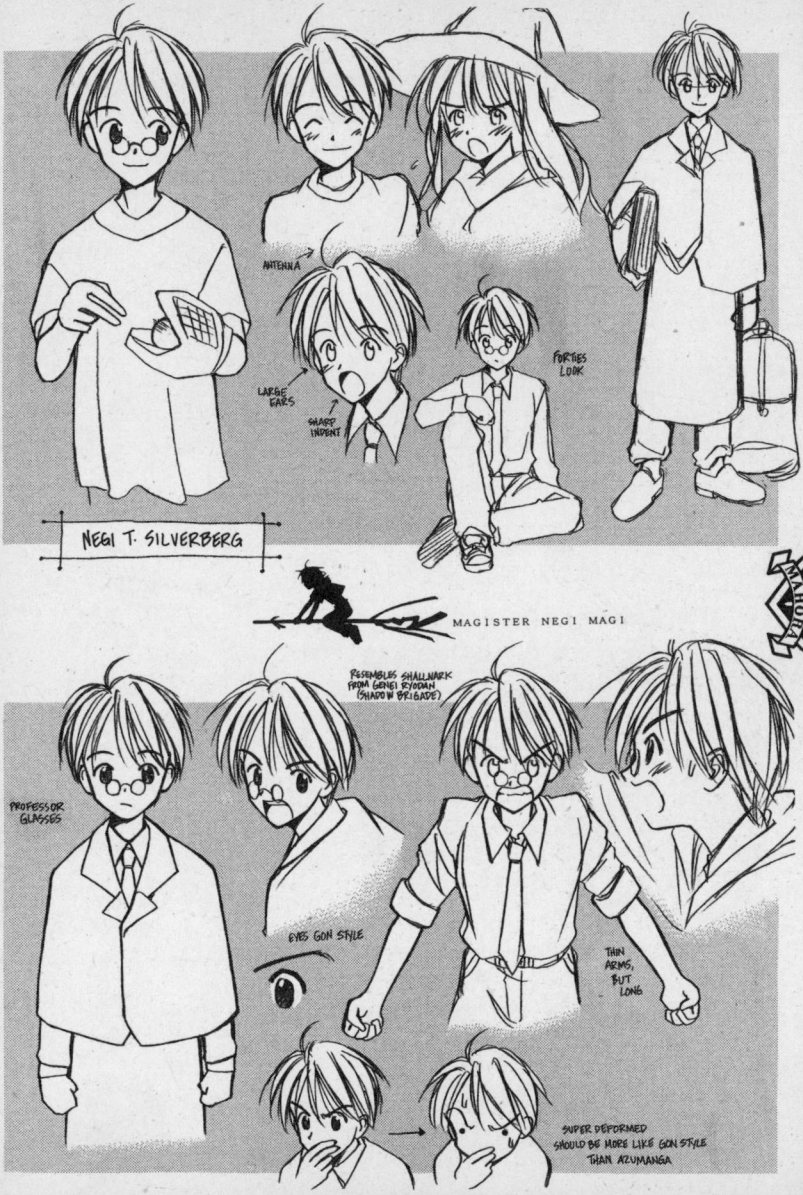
ANTENNA
LARGE EARS
SHARP INDENT
FORTIES LOOK
NEGI T. SILVERBERG
MAGISTER NEGI MAGI
RESEMBLES SHALLWARK FROM GENEI RYODAN (SHADOW BRIGADE)
PROFESSOR GLASSES
EYES GON STYLE
THIN ARMS, BUT LONG
SUPER DEFORMED SHOULD BE MORE LIKE GON STYLE THAN AZUMANGA

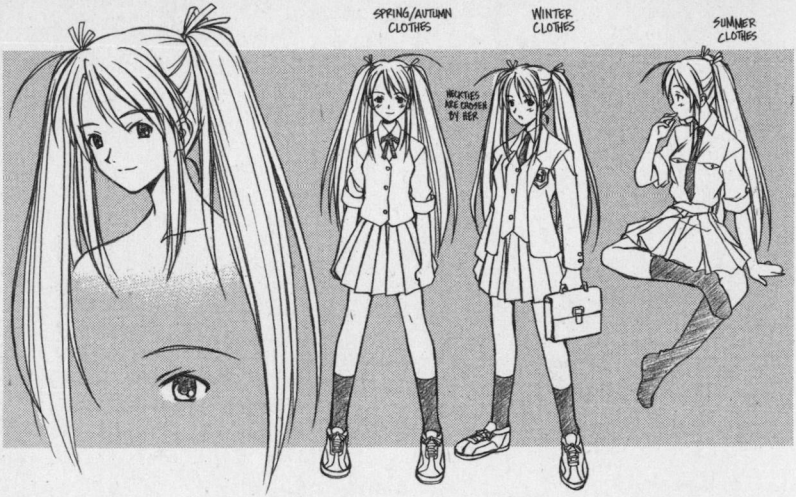

AZUNA KAGURAZAKA

THE CONCEPT ART FOR THE MALE AND FEMALE PROTAGONIST. NEGI'S LIKE, "WHAT?!" (^^;) WE ENDED UP REJECTING THIS VERSION, OPTING FOR A MORE CHILDISH, ROUND FACED CHARACTER.
HE IS CUTER THAT WAY AFTER ALL ~ ♡

THE FEMALE PROTAGONIST IS BASICALLY TAKEN FROM A HEROINE CHARACTER FROM A CANCELLED PROJECT I WAS WORKING ON BEFORE "NEGIMA". THESE TWO ARE LIKE SIBLINGS, SO MAYBE IT'S A LITTLE ODD AS A LOVE COMEDY?

PROTAGONIST'S ADVISOR-
SHIZUNA-SENSEI (30)

SHE SHOULD WEAR CLOTHES LIKE THIS OUTFIT.

YOU CAN'T HELP BUT NOTICE THIS AREA.

MATERNAL LOOK

LARGE BREASTS. REALLY BIG. WIDE HIPS TOO, BUT HER WAIST IS THIN.

BUT SHE HAS A CHILD THE SAME AGE AS THE PROTAGONIST! (SO SHE CAN'T HELP BUT GIVE THE PROTAGONIST HER LOVING CARE.)

MAGISTER NEGI MAGI

EVERY ONE OF THE 31 CLASSMATES HAVE THEIR OWN DETAILED CONCEPT DESIGNS, BUT RIGHT NOW I CAN'T PROVIDE A CHARACTER DESIGN CHART... SO I'LL START WITH SHIZUNA-SENSEI WHO DOESN'T HAVE MUCH OF A DETAILED CONCEPT DESIGN (HA HA)

I WONDER WHAT KIND OF RELATIONSHIP SHE HAS WITH TAKAHATA-SENSEI?

(* WE HAVE DECIDED THAT SHE DOESN'T HAVE CHILDREN AFTER ALL.)

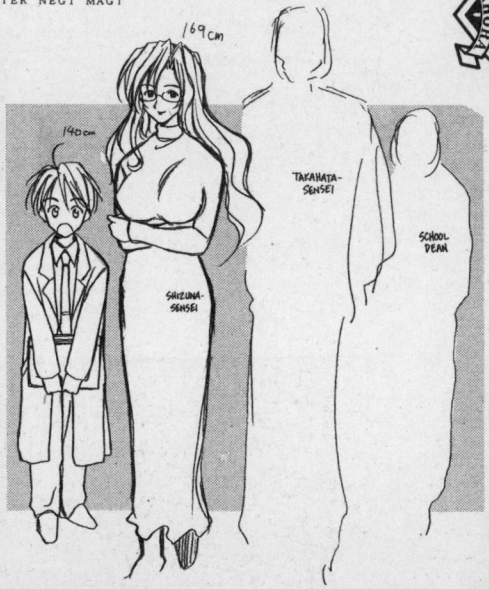

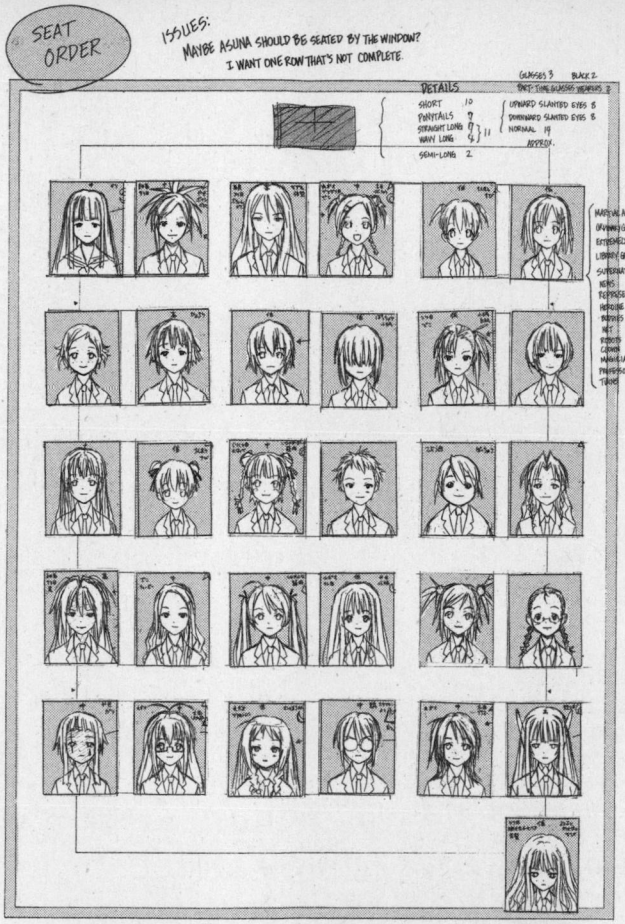

NEXT, WE'LL BE SHOWING THE CLASSMATE CONCEPT DESIGNS ~ (^^).
MAYBE YOUR FAVORITE GAL WILL SHOW UP. SEE YOU IN VOLUME 2 THEN!

Translation Notes

Japanese is a tricky language for most westerners, and translation is often more art than science. For your edification and reading pleasure, here are notes on some of the places where we could have gone in a different direction in our translation of the work, or where a Japanese cultural reference is used.

If you're reading all of the manga from the launch (and if you're not, go pick up *Gundam SEED*, *xxxHOLiC*, and *Tsubasa* right now!), you'll have seen that we've gone to great effort to keep our translations as authentic as possible. Nowhere did that pose such a challenge, however, as with *Negima!*

Two decisions we made early on in planning the line were to maintain Japanese honorifics as appropriate (for example, if a manga were set in, say, America, there would be little point in keeping them), and to translate all sound effects. We've managed to do both of these things in all of our books, but *Negima!* has been the most—shall we say—troublesome.

To begin with, take a look through the book at all of the sound effects. Akamatsu-sensei sure does like to use them, doesn't he? Where in our other manga we were experiencing 0 to 5 sound effects per page, with several pages lacking effects entirely, *Negima!* has more like 2 to 10 effects and asides per page! As difficult as it was to translate them all (and I'm not certain, but it's possible we managed to miss some along the way), *Negima!* highlights why it is so necessary to do the extra translation work and provide the reader with a more complete, immersive reading experience.

While honorifics came up in our other manga, they were definitely a major necessity in *Negima!* because it takes place in a school—a very formal setting in Japan. An understanding of Japanese honorifics drives home the relationships between the characters. Look at when Negi first runs into Takahata—he calls him by his first name with no honorific at all, clearly indicating they are good friends.

Likewise, when Takahata interrupts Asuna and Negi after school, he calls them both Asuna-kun and Negi-kun, which to Negi should indicate friendship, while to Asuna it's simply an acknowledgment that she is a student and Takahata is a teacher.

Preview of Volume 2

Because we're running about one year behind the release of the Japanese *Negima!* manga, we have the opportunity to present to you a preview from Volume 2. This volume will be available in English in August 2004, but for now you'll have to make do with Japanese!

チュンチュン

★この物語はフィクションです。実在の人物、団体名等とは関係ありません。

ふわ〜〜〜あ そろそろあったかくなってきたね——

そーですねこのかさん

二人ともしゃべってないで走りなさいよ 遅刻するわよー

ドドドッ

ネギ君おっはよー

やっほ——ネギ先生♡

あ 佐々木さんに和泉さん！

おはよ——

こないだのドッジボール面白かったねー

またやろ！

スカッとしたわ

ハハハ そーですねー

キーン コーン カーン

おはよー ネギ先生

ネギ君 おはよー♡

あ おはよー こざいます

オーッス♡ ネギぼーずー

オーッス♡

みんなの挨拶 うれしいな…… なんか最近 先生として 受け入れられてる つぽいし……

この分なら けっこう簡単に 立派な魔法使いに なれるかも……!?

中等部二年A組

ワイ ワイ

じゃあ 今のところを 訳してもらいます

NEO HORIZON

え～～～と ……

じゃあ朝元気に挨拶してくれた佐々木さん！

アハハハハ

ガタッ

えー——ネギ君ひどいー挨拶して損した——っ

ネギ先生訳なら私が……！

じいんちょハーフだからだめー

なっ……ハーフじゃありませんわよ

ワイワイ

アハハ

……

彼にはもう一つ課題をクリアしてもらおうかの
才能ある立派な魔法使いの候補生として——
——ん？
ワイワイ
ザワ
ザワ
ピリ
ピリ
…何か他のクラスのみなさんピリピリしてますね——
あ——そだね
そろそろ中等部の期末テストが近いからね
来週の月曜からだよネギ君

へ――学期末テストですかあ
大変だあ

…って
2―Aもそうなのでは!?
のんびりしていいんですか!!
ビシャン
あ――
あはは うちの学校エスカレーター式だからあんまり関係ないんだ

特に2―Aはずーっと学年最下位だけど大丈夫大丈夫
ミ～マイ～♡
はうう
大丈夫じゃないでしょあんまり～～～
てへ

…？あのお花みたいなトロフィーは？
あー あれはテストで学年トップになったクラスがもらえるんだよ
へ――

そっか――…2―Aは学年最下位だったのか――
なんとかした方がいいのかな…
あんなトロフィー欲しいけど無理かな？無理だな…

いや…確かそーゆー時に効く魔法が何かあったような…
――ネギ先生
あ はい!?
しずな先生
ぶつぶつ
ぴくっ

あの…学園長先生がこれをあなたにって…
え…何ですか深刻な顔して

えっ!? 僕への最終課題!?

ネギ教育実習生 最終課題

あわわっ!? 今頃こんな課題が出るなんて聞いてなかったよー!?

たったた大変だっ!

攻撃魔法200個取得!?

悪のドラゴン退治!?

これをクリアしないと正式な先生にも立派な魔法使いにもなれなくなっちゃうー!?

ドキドキドキドキ

ピラッ…

……どんな課題なんだろ……?

ねぎ君へ
次の期末試験で、
二ーAが最下位脱出できたら
正式な先生にしてあげる。

麻帆良学園学園長　近衛近右衛門

どーーん

なっ……

期末で最下位脱出!?

COLLECT ALL FOUR SERIES FROM DEL REY!

▌First time in the U.S.! ▌Printed in the authentic Japanese style! ▌Bonus materials inside!

Tsubasa: RESERVoir CHRoNiCLE
by CLAMP

Negima!
by Ken Akamatsu

xxxHOLiC
by CLAMP

Gundam SEED
by Masatsugu Iwase, Hajime Yatate, and Yoshiyuki Tomino

For more information and to sign up for Del Rey's manga e-newsletter, visit www.delreymanga.com

Gundam SEED © 2004 Hajime Yatate, Yoshiyuki Tomino and Masatsugu Iwase. All rights reserved. © Sotsu Agency, Sunrise, MBS. First published in Japan in 2004 by Kodansha Ltd., Tokyo. The publication rights arranged through Kodansha Ltd. NEGIMA ©2003 Ken Akamatsu. All rights reserved. TSUBASA ©2003 CLAMP. All rights reserved. xxxHOLiC © 2003 CLAMP. All rights reserved.

xxxHOLiC

by CLAMP

Creators of *Chobits!*

Watanuki Kimihiro is haunted by visions of ghosts and spirits. Seemingly by chance, he encounters a mysterious witch named Yuko, who claims she can help. In desperation, he accepts, but realizes that he's just been tricked into working for Yuko in order to pay off the cost of her services. Soon he's employed in her little shop—a job which turns out to be nothing like his previous work experience!

Most of Yuko's customers live in Japan, but Yuko and Watanuki are about to have some unusual visitors named Sakura and Syaoran from a land called Clow. . . .

Volume 1: On sale May 2004 • Volume 2: On sale July 2004
Volume 3: On sale November 2004

For more information and to sign up for Del Rey's manga e-newsletter, visit www.delreymanga.com

xxxHOLiC © 2003 CLAMP. All rights reserved.

Tsubasa: RESERVoir CHRoNiCLE by CLAMP

Sakura and Syaoran return! But they're not the people you know. Sakura is the princess of Clow—and possessor of a mysterious, misunderstood power that promises to change the world. Syaoran is her childhood friend, and leader of the archaeological dig that took his father's life. They reside in an alternate reality . . . where whatever you least expect can happen—and does. When Sakura ventures to the dig site to declare her love for Syaoran, a puzzling symbol is uncovered—which triggers a remarkable quest. Now Syaoran embarks upon a desperate journey through the worlds of *X*, *Chobits*, *Magic Knight Rayearth*, *xxxHOLiC* and many more classic CLAMP series. All in the name of Syaoran's single goal: saving Sakura.

Volume 1: On sale May 2004 • Volume 2: On sale September 2004
Volume 3: On sale December 2004

For more information and to sign up for Del Rey's manga e-newsletter, visit www.delreymanga.com

TSUBASA © 2003 CLAMP. All rights reserved.

Gundam SEED

by Masatsugu Iwase, Hajime Yatate, and Yoshiyuki Tomino

In the world of the Cosmic Era, a war is underway between the genetically enhanced humans known as Coordinators and those who remain unmodified, called Naturals. The Natural-dominated Earth Alliance, struggling to catch up with the Coordinators' superior technology, has secretly developed its own Gundam mobile suits at a neutral space colony. But through a twist of fate, a young Coordinator named Kira Yamato becomes the pilot of the Alliance's prototype Strike Gundam, and finds himself forced to fight his own people in order to protect his friends. Featuring all the best elements of the legendary Gundam saga, this thrilling new series reimagines the gripping story of men, women, and magnificent fighting machines in epic conflict.

Volume 1: On sale May 2004 • Volume 2: On sale September 2004

DEL REY

For more information and to sign up for Del Rey's manga e-newsletter, visit www.delreymanga.com

Gundam SEED © 2004 Hajime Yatate, Yoshiyuki Tomino and Masatsugu Iwase. All rights reserved.
© Sotsu Agency, Sunrise, MBS. First published in Japan in 2004 by Kodansha Ltd., Tokyo.
The publication rights arranged through Kodansha Ltd.

TOMARE!

[STOP!]

You're going the wrong way!

Manga is a completely different type of reading experience.

To start at the *beginning*, go to the *end*!

That's right! Authentic manga is read the traditional Japanese way—from right to left. Exactly the *opposite* of how American books are read. It's easy to follow: Just go to the other end of the book, and read each page—and each panel—from right side to left side, starting at the top right. Now you're experiencing manga as it was meant to be.